"What are we going to do with an abandoned baby on Christmas Eve?"

"I suppose one of us could drive her to San Antonio," suggested the police officer who'd come to the scene.

"And do *what* with her once you get there?" Heather asked.

Shawn thought he detected an edge of panic in her voice and discreetly narrowed his eyes on the local foster mother.

Yes, there it was. She was afraid for this baby. So was Shawn.

"I just can't help but feel this baby was sent to us, to our town, to this church," he said.

To me. He wasn't about to say those words out loud, but he was certainly thinking about them.

"If we're not going to take Noelle to San Antonio tonight," the officer said, "then what are we going to do with her?"

Shawn took a deep breath and stepped out onto the high wire, knowing there was no net below him. He stared into the stormy blue-eyed gaze of baby Noelle.

"I'll take care of her."

Books by Deb Kastner

Love Inspired

A Holiday Prayer
Daddy's Home
Black Hills Bride
The Forgiving Heart
A Daddy at Heart
A Perfect Match
The Christmas Groom
Hart's Harbor
Undercover Blessings
The Heart of a Man
A Wedding in Wyoming
His Texas Bride

The Marine's Baby
A Colorado Match
*Phoebe's Groom
*The Doctor's Secret Son
*The Nanny's Twin Blessings
*Meeting Mr. Right
†The Soldier's Sweetheart
†Her Valentine Sheriff
†Redeeming the Rancher
◊Yuletide Baby

*Email Order Brides
†Serendipity Sweethearts
◊Cowboy Country

DEB KASTNER

lives and writes in colorful Colorado with the Front Range of the Rocky Mountains for inspiration. She loves writing for Love Inspired Books, where she can write about her two favorite things—faith and love. Her characters range from upbeat and humorous to (her favorite) dark and broody heroes. Her plots fall anywhere in between, from a playful romp to the deeply emotional. Deb's books have been twice nominated for the RT Reviewers' Choice Award for Best Book of the Year for Love Inspired. Deb and her husband share their home with their two youngest daughters. Deb is thrilled about the newest member of the family—her first granddaughter, Isabella. What fun to be a granny! Deb loves to hear from her readers. You can contact her by email at DEBWRTR@aol.com, or on her MySpace or Facebook pages.

Yuletide Baby

Deb Kastner

HARLEQUIN® LOVE INSPIRED®

Recycling programs for this product may not exist in your area.

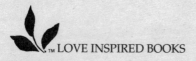 ™ LOVE INSPIRED BOOKS

ISBN-13: 978-0-373-81807-5

Yuletide Baby

Through the Lord's mercies we are not consumed,
Because His compassions fail not.
They are new every morning,
Great is Your faithfulness,
"The Lord is my portion," says my soul,
Therefore I hope in Him.
—*Lamentations* 3:22–24

To Alex and Annie Baer.
May God bless your marriage in every way,
and may your love for one another grow stronger
every day. Love to you both, and Izzie, too!

Chapter One

Silent night. Holy night.

Pastor Shawn O'Riley pulled in a deep breath, savoring the rich combination of scents. Poinsettias and evergreens.

Christmas.

He relished the deep peace of the now-empty chapel and was grateful for the blessed evening, although he was equally glad it was finished. Christmas Eve for a pastor could be rather stressful, especially for a simple cowboy preacher who worked on the land for a living and pastored the little church part-time. He'd mended as many literal fences for the neighbors as he had spiritual ones, but he loved every second of it—all of it. Especially, on a night like tonight.

Not many knew of all the behind-the-scenes effort needed to pull the more complicated church services together. The children's nativity pageant had gone off without a hitch—give or take a few easily distracted preschool-aged angels and a donkey who couldn't stand still long enough to recite his single line. The parents had loved it and the children had enjoyed performing, and that was all that really mattered to Shawn.

Following that had been the Christmas Eve midnight service, which was one of his favorites, starting with beloved carols and ending in the tranquility of candlelight.

All is calm. All is bright.

And it was. The atmosphere couldn't be more silent and serene. So why did he have a niggling deep in his gut that something was wrong?

He scoffed softly and shook his head. It had been a long week, between preparing some of his animals for the big stock sale coming just after the first of the year and organizing the Christmas Eve festivities. He was overtired, it was as simple as that. There wasn't any deeper significance to whatever unease he was feeling. If he had any sense he'd stop standing here straining for sounds that didn't exist and head back to his ranch so he could get himself to bed where he belonged. Settle in for a long winter's nap, and all that.

Before heading out, all he had left to do was

make sure all the lights were off, the candles blown out and the doors locked, and then he could go home.

Alone. To an empty house.

Was that the real reason he lingered?

It wasn't the first time he would be spending Christmas Eve on his own, and he was sure that it wouldn't be his last, but for some reason he was feeling it more than usual. He hadn't spent Christmas with his family since— Well, he didn't want to think about that.

He shook his head to unsettle the disturbing sense of melancholy. He *wasn't* alone. He might be feeling a little lonely, but the Lord was always with him. God had seen him through many a Christmas past.

With a weary sigh, he flipped all seven switches on the light plate, plunging the vestibule into darkness and leaving only the soft flickering of candles beckoning from the warmth of the sanctuary. He'd forgotten to extinguish them.

Shawn grunted and combed his fingers through the short tips of his reddish-blond hair and ran a hand across the five-o'clock shadow on his jaw. Just as well that he had to head back into the sanctuary to take care of the candles. It would give him a moment to refocus and shake this unexpected despondency, remind himself that feelings weren't everything. God was always his comfort and consolation, whether Shawn could feel Him or not.

The light beckoned him. He removed his cowboy hat from his head as he passed through the familiar arch that marked the entrance to the sanctuary. Reverently, and with a catch in his throat, he approached the altar.

He'd been given so many blessings. His health. A little spread of land he was proud to call his own. His six-year ministry at a chapel he adored in a town full of folks he loved. He hadn't been born in Serendipity, and yet the community had welcomed him with open arms as one of their own.

He had so much for which to be grateful. How could he possibly complain when many people were blessed with far less?

As he reached the foot of the altar, he knelt, his eyes dropping from the large wooden cross centered on the wall to the straw-stuffed manger the children had used during the pageant. He grinned as he recalled squalling *Baby Jesus*, Eli and Mary Bishop's newborn son. The little nipper had squirmed so hard the entire manger—

Something moved within the straw.

Shawn blinked and rubbed his eyes. What *was* that?

He must be more exhausted than he'd realized. For a moment there he was positive he'd seen—

There it was again.

From the manger. Just the tiniest quiver within the stalks of hay, as if a whisper of a breeze had passed over it.

Only there was no breeze in the chapel.

A shiver ran up his spine as he bolted to his feet and took an involuntary step backward. The candlelight was no help, casting shadows across the walls and floor. His heart hammering in his throat, Shawn approached the crèche.

When he leaned in to see what had caused the disturbance, his eyes widened and his breath tugged.

A *baby.*

A real-live newborn infant, loosely wrapped—not in swaddling clothes, but in a tattered Dallas Cowboys snug-wrap blanket. As Shawn watched, the infant's face scrunched as if it were about to break into a wail, but then just as swiftly its expression relaxed back into the peace of sleep.

Adrenaline surged through Shawn, erasing whatever fatigue and anxiety he'd been combating moments before. His mind went into overdrive with a brand-new kind of worry. He was fearful to move, even to breathe.

What was going on here? This couldn't be

happening. Not in this little church, in a small town in the middle of nowhere, and not on Christmas Eve. He rubbed his eyes with his thumb and forefinger, but when he glanced back down at the manger, the baby was still very much present.

Real. Alive. And kicking.

The hair on the back of his neck prickled as his mind raced to take in the facts, what few there were. Where was the baby's mother? Shawn cast a glance around the sanctuary, but there were no additional movements in the darkness. Somehow, the woman had come and gone without him even knowing she'd ever been.

And she'd left behind the most precious of cargo.

He knew he didn't have any new or expectant moms in the congregation, other than Mary Bishop. To Shawn's untrained eye, all newborns looked like Yoda, but he was certain this wasn't the same little guy who'd played Baby Jesus. He'd watched Eli and Mary pack up their little bundle and exit the church an hour earlier.

Come to think of it, he wasn't even sure the baby presently lying in the manger was a little *guy*.

The infant's eyes popped open, revealing an unfocused smoky blue-gray gaze. Shawn reached out a finger and the infant grasped it, pulling his hand toward its tiny mouth. Despite all the tension he was feeling, Shawn couldn't help but smile softly as he slid his large palm underneath the baby's head and tenderly scooped it into his arms. Babies were blessings from God, plain and simple.

Only, in this case, the *plain and simple* part of it was a little more complicated. He hoped he was doing this "cradling the baby" thing right. He was hardly an expert on the subject. He was supposed to support the baby's head and neck—that much he remembered from christenings. With this little one, it wasn't hard to do. The infant was so tiny it almost fit into one of his large palms.

"Shh, shh, shh," he murmured gently to the whimpering infant. He rocked on the heels of his boots. "It's okay, little one. I've got you. Everything's going to be okay. I promise."

He frowned. That wasn't exactly right. Not that the baby could understand his words, but he was hardly in a position to make a promise like that. There wasn't one single thing about this situation that was *okay*.

Where was the mother now? How had she gotten into the church and back out again without anyone noticing her? Had she disappeared for good, or was she lingering around somewhere to make sure her baby was well cared for? Had she picked this chapel for a reason, out of all the places she could have taken the child?

And maybe the most pressing question of all—what was *he* supposed to do with an abandoned baby on Christmas Eve?

If he wasn't mistaken, there were safe-haven laws in Texas to deal with the issue of child abandonment, but Shawn didn't know the exact details. Would a church even be considered an acceptable drop-off point in such a situation? Perhaps allowances could be made, since the nearest hospital was over an hour away? And speaking of hospitals, he should call Delia Bowden, the town doctor, who would no doubt want to check the baby's health. Also, he would need to call the police immediately, to report what could potentially be considered a crime.

He forced a breath through his lungs. He had people who'd help him through this. That was a good thing. But the question remained—whom should he call first? No matter how he tried to reason around it, he couldn't get over the fact that whatever motivations had compelled the woman to commit such an act, the distressed mother had chosen to leave her precious baby *here*, in this church, and not at the police station or firehouse as she might have done.

A myriad of emotions pressed upon him and he struggled to work them out, to untie the knots in his chest. There had to be a reason the baby was here. God didn't make mistakes, and though it seemed incomprehensible to Shawn, it was abundantly clear to him that *he* was meant to find this child.

But why?

Threading his fingers through his hair, he murmured a frantic prayer for guidance under his breath. What would the Lord have him do?

Jo Spencer. Owner of Cup O' Jo Café and second mother to half the town, she had a word of advice to give for any situation under the sun. She'd been a good listening ear and friendly adviser to him in the past.

It was a decision, at least, and a good one, at that. He sighed in relief.

Jo would know what to do in his hour of need. She was the resident expert on everything—and everyone. Shawn was reluctant to wake her at this time of night, but he knew she would want to be part of this. At the very least, she'd help him think through his options, and she'd definitely know who else to call in as reinforcements. She quite literally knew everyone in town. She might even have an idea who the mother was. If there were any women outside the church's parish who might be pregnant and close to delivery, Jo would know about them.

Shawn's heart ached for the woman who was

desperate enough to leave her infant at a church on Christmas Eve. She must be feeling such a deep sense of anguish. No doubt her circumstances, whatever they were, had been dire.

He shifted and wrinkled his nose as an odd, pungent odor assaulted him.

"Yes, little person," he said, addressing the baby. "We need to call in the cavalry."

Along with everything else, Jo Spencer would know how to change a diaper.

He curled the infant into one arm and fished for his cell phone in the pocket of his black slacks. Fortunately, Jo was an active member of the faith community, and her number was on speed dial.

After several rings, a gravelly, sleep-muted male voice answered.

"This'd better be good." Jo's husband, Frank, was gruff on the best of occasions, and Shawn highly doubted that being dragged from a dead sleep even remotely qualified for that category.

"So sorry to wake you, Frank, but I've got a bit of an emergency here. This is Pastor Shawn, by the way."

"Yeah, I figured. When Jo's new-fangled cell phone rang, your picture came up on the screen."

One corner of Shawn's mouth rose. He heard a crackle and a thump on the other end of the line.

"Emergency, you said?" Jo didn't even sound sleepy, though he knew he'd wakened her from the same state that had Frank so grumpy. "What can I do for you, Pastor?"

Shawn released the breath he'd been holding, relief rippling through his muscles as he continued to jiggle his arm to keep the gurgling infant happy.

"I have a baby," he blurted.

"Oh. I…" It was unusual for Jo to stammer. He'd clearly caught her off guard, and no wonder. "Are congratulations in order?"

"What?" Of all the things he expected Jo to say, that wasn't it. "No. I mean— It's not *my* baby."

Jo let out a big guffaw. Shawn wondered how anyone could sound so gleeful in the middle of the night.

"Well, young man, you'll pardon me for sayin' I'm relieved to hear it. Not that you wouldn't make a wonderful father, mind."

"Thank you for that," he responded, chuckling under his breath. "But I do have a problem. That baby I mentioned—I have it right here. At the church. I think someone abandoned it." He hated calling the baby an *it*, but he thought calling Jo was more expedient than taking the time to check to see if it was a boy or a girl.

"Oh, my stars," Jo exclaimed. "An abandoned baby? Well, why didn't you say so to begin with?"

Shawn grimaced and the baby startled, wagging his or her little arms in the air and breaking into a weak wail.

"I hear the dear little sweetheart. Is it a boy or a girl?"

Shawn shifted the wiggling bundle to his shoulder and bounced softly on his toes. "I don't know. I haven't checked yet. I called you first."

"And that was exactly the right thing for you to do, my dear. I'll be over faster than you can say *Jack Washington*. We'll figure it out together, you and I. I do believe I'll also get on the horn with Heather Lewis and see if she can come out and help us."

"Heather Lewis?"

"She's a local foster parent. I imagine she'll be able to give us some perspective on the situation."

With an inaudible sigh, Shawn crooked the phone against his shoulder so he could pat the infant on the back. Jo had no idea how very much he needed to hear that help was on its way. What he knew about babies was quite literally limited to the christenings he performed. He didn't have any children of his own, nor did he have nieces or nephews. He'd never actually had to *care* for a baby before, especially not in the plethora of ways he imagined this little one would need.

Apprehension shot through him like a bolt of electricity, crackling and exploding along every one of his nerve endings. He wasn't qualified to be in charge of a child. He hadn't even been successful watching an older kid, much less a newborn. He closed his eyes and saw his younger brother David's face, red and sweating, his palms pressed against the glass of the car door and his mouth open in a silent scream.

No. Not now.

Pain stabbed through his gut, and he opened his eyes wide, gasping for air.

Please, Lord, let Jo come quickly.

"I can't tell you what this means to me. Thank you. From the bottom of my heart." *And then some.*

"No need to thank me, son. That's what I'm here for—helpin' people as the Lord sees fit to use me." He knew she told the truth. It didn't matter that it was the middle of the night or Christmas Eve. Jo was happy to be everyone's go-to woman.

"Hey, Jo?" he asked when the infant's face once again scrunched, turning from peach to red to an alarming shade of purple.

"Yes, dear?"

"You think you could possibly rustle up a clean diaper while you're at it?"

Jo chuckled. "Don't worry, dear. I'll bring supplies. We're going to manage just fine. Mark my words—everything is going to work out. For all of us."

What Shawn wouldn't give to have Jo's faith right now. He wasn't quite so certain about how things were going to work out, particularly for this precious child. All he knew for sure was that this long night was about to get longer.

Persistent pounding drew Heather Lewis from sleep so deep that she thought she was dreaming the noise—or that perhaps the pounding was just the headache that had set in earlier. She groaned and rolled over, covering her head with her feather pillow. With all the excitement of Christmas Eve, she hadn't managed to get her little brood to bed until late. Exhaustion weighed down every bone and muscle in her body.

Though muted by her pillow, the hammering continued. *Rap, rap, rap.* Pause. *Rap, rap, rap.*

Suddenly she sat bolt upright, adrenaline pumping through her veins and bringing her to instant alertness as she thrashed around, trying to release her legs from the blanket she was caught up in.

She wasn't dreaming about those sharp knocks. They were real. Her mind shrieked in terror.

Run. Hide.

She clutched the neck of her flannel pajamas as her pulse raged through her, her nerve endings screaming and shattering.

Adrian.

No. She shook her sleep-muddled head. *Not Adrian.*

Adrian was in prison in Colorado, and he had been for years. She had recently returned to her hometown in Serendipity, Texas—far, far away from the nightmare she'd once lived. She was safe.

She tucked her forehead against her knees and gulped for air, a sob of relief escaping her lips.

She was okay. She was okay.

She repeated the mantra even as the pounding on the door resumed.

"Heather?" The voice coming from the other side of the door was a woman's, and though she sounded urgent, there wasn't an ounce of threat in her tone.

Heather rolled to her feet and padded to the front door, taking a quick glance through the peephole for final reassurance before opening up.

"Jo?" she asked, surprised to see the boisterous owner of the local café on her doorstep in the middle of the night. "What's wrong?"

"I tried calling but you didn't pick up."

"I'm sorry. I mute my phone at night so it won't wake up the little ones." She pressed Jo's wringing hands. Something had to be seriously wrong for Jo to be here this late, and on Christmas Eve, to boot. "Do you want to come in?"

"Thank you, dear." Jo followed Heather inside. "I hate to impose on you, especially at this hour, but I'm in desperate need of your assistance."

"Sure. Anything. Whatever you need." Heather didn't hesitate. Growing up in Serendipity, she'd spent many happy hours at Cup O' Jo Café, leaning on the advice of the ever-wise Jo Spencer. Heather couldn't imagine why Jo needed her help, but it was a given that she'd do anything she could.

"A baby has been abandoned at the church. Pastor Shawn is quite flabbergasted by the event, as well you can imagine. Seeing as we don't have a social worker here in town, I figured you were the next best thing, being a foster mother and all. You'll come with me to see to the little one, won't you? I already phoned your next-door neighbor, and she'll be here shortly to make sure your kiddos are looked after while you're gone."

"We're going to the chapel?" Heather was truly ready to do anything—except that. The shiver that overtook her rocked her to the very core. She hadn't stepped through the door of a church in years, and she never wanted to do so again. Not for as long as she lived. Her stomach lurched with the thought, and the fear was paralyzing.

She opened her mouth to decline, but closed it without speaking, rubbing her lips together as she considered her options. There was a sweet, innocent baby to think about. She'd made a promise to herself that if she was presented with the opportunity, she'd be there for any and all children in need.

But this? She squeezed her eyes closed and swallowed her trepidation, searching for her resolve.

"Give me a minute to get dressed," she said to Jo before walking back to the bedroom. She needed the time, not just to change clothes, but to decide if she was really up to this.

She slipped into jeans and a blue cotton pullover and stooped to lace her sneakers, her mind still in turmoil.

Could she do it? Would she be able to overcome years of terror and defensiveness to help the little one?

For the baby's sake, she had to try.

Once her next-door neighbor had arrived to watch the children, Heather and Jo set off. The drive from Heather's house to the chapel was only a few short minutes, but to Heather the distance seemed agonizingly long. Jo bustled out of her old truck the moment she parked it. Heather held back, clutching her hands together in her lap as she gathered her courage. After what felt like an hour but was probably no more than a few seconds, she forced herself to exit the vehicle. A wave of dizziness immediately overtook her and she grasped at the rim of the truck to keep her balance.

Air in. Air out, she coaxed herself. When these panic attacks hit, her breath came in shallow gasps and she hyperventilated, resulting in the light-headedness she was now experiencing. She was so…*angry* that she couldn't control her reactions. It was embarrassing. Humiliating.

"Heather, are you coming?" Jo had made it up to the chapel's red double doors before she glanced back and realized Heather wasn't following her. The old red-headed woman's face instantly crumpled with concern. "What is it, dear?"

Suppressing a shiver, Heather straightened

her shoulders and picked up the box of baby paraphernalia from the back of Jo's truck.

She forced a smile. "I'm sorry I'm being so slow. Don't worry. I'll be in right behind you."

While in essence, that was true, emotionally, Heather was lagging, and she was painfully aware of why.

The chapel is just a building, she scolded herself sternly. If anything, this particular chapel was a place of happy childhood memories. But she couldn't seem to separate the structure from the experiences in her past. The thought of church—any church—was tainted by the thought of Adrian, who had been a beloved and highly respected deacon. No one had realized that it had all been one big lie.

This guy isn't Adrian.

Truthfully, she didn't know anything about the pastor she was here to assist. There was no reason for her to believe Shawn O'Riley would be in any way similar to Adrian, other than being a part of the active leadership of a church. It was wrong to judge all men on a single man's faults, but she couldn't seem to help herself. In her experience, men said one thing and did another. And what they did was bad. It was *bad*. All of her self-preserving instincts were screaming at her to run fast and far away from this situation.

She knew it wasn't logical. This place, Serendipity's little white chapel, was the church she'd grown up in, a place of warm memories and happy times. It was where she'd first learned to sing "Jesus Loves Me," where she'd been told she was His little lamb and that if she became lost, He would cheerfully leave all of His other sheep to come and find her.

Only, when she'd become lost, no one had come to find her, not even the Lord.

And that was just one more grudge to hold against Adrian—one more way in which he'd hurt her. This place, that used to stand for security and love, now just made her anxious and uncomfortable. There was no safety to be found here. Not for her. Nor was there a chance of trust on her part to be given to any man who had a hand in running it. Just the thought of meeting the pastor made her stomach twist.

If she had a lick of sense she'd turn right around and go home. This wasn't her battle.

If it weren't for this baby...

But there *was* a baby. That infant *made* it her battle. She'd promised Jo she would help, and that alone would have been enough to keep her walking forward. But more than that, she'd made a personal vow that she would help children in need wherever and whenever she found them. She couldn't make up for what Adrian had done—and she could never fully forgive herself for what she had stepped aside and *allowed* him to do—but maybe, just maybe, she could help someone else's child, like this tiny gift of humanity who had apparently been horribly abandoned by the very people who should have loved him or her the most.

She'd help the baby, she'd do whatever Jo needed her to do—and then she'd leave the chapel, and the pastor she had no interest in knowing, behind.

As she entered the church and was greeted by Pastor Shawn, it was all she could do not to recoil from his handshake. Oh, he appeared pleasant enough with his Irish good looks—reddish-blond hair, a kind expression on his face and laugh lines fanning from his light blue eyes. Both his gaze and his smile were welcoming. He was obviously relieved that support had arrived. But Heather knew how easy it was for a man to put on a mask for the world and hide his true nature. A charming smile no longer had the capacity to fool her. Especially not on a preacher.

"Jo. Ma'am." He tipped his head toward Heather. "Thank you both for coming in the middle of the night."

"This is Heather Lewis," Jo said by way of introduction. "She's our resident expert, seeing as she has a house full of foster children.

She also has a professional background in child care, which I suspect will be invaluable to us."

As small as Serendipity was, Pastor Shawn had probably heard her name, just as she knew his, but up until now they'd had no reason to cross paths. He wasn't a native of Serendipity and had become the pastor of the small congregation a couple years after Heather had left town for college, where she'd met and eventually married Adrian. And she'd certainly never even remotely considered darkening the door of his church upon her return.

"Thank you, thank you. I'm happy for any help I can get. I couldn't believe it when I found— Well, here. Come with me and I'll show you."

Shawn's stride was long and confident as he led them up the sanctuary aisle to where a life-size crèche beckoned. Heather's heart leaped when she saw the tiny infant lying in the manger, swaddled in what looked to be a tattered football blanket. She wondered if the baby had been left that way by the mother, or if the blanket was Shawn's touch.

"Oh, the poor little dear," Jo exclaimed, wasting no time in scooping the baby into her arms.

"He fell asleep, so I placed him back in the manger. Or her—I don't really know yet. It seemed like a safe spot, as close to a crib as I have available. As you can see, I'm way out of my league here."

"I can't even begin to imagine how you felt when you discovered the babe," Jo agreed, kissing the now-squirming infant's forehead. "And this is how you found him? Er—her? All wrapped up in this blanket?" Jo turned and thrust the baby toward Heather. "Heather, dear, can you help me get this poor little thing's diaper changed and get the boy/girl thing settled for us? I am already weary of referring to him/her in a double-gender fashion."

Heather accepted the infant and sat down on the front pew to change the child. It wasn't the most ideal of conditions, but at this point the baby's needs and comfort were more important than the propriety of the church setting.

"It's a girl," she informed them as she re-swaddled the infant, this time in a soft, clean pink receiving blanket she'd brought along in her stash of baby things, leftovers from her previous career as a day-care provider.

"A girl," Shawn repeated, his gaze tender and his voice full of wonder. "How about that?" From the bemused expression on his face and the way his warm voice dipped in awe, she might have thought he'd never seen a newborn baby before. Maybe it was just the shock of the situation that had thrown him.

"The poor mother," Jo breathed, placing an empathetic hand over her heart. "I can't imagine what she must be feeling right now, to have abandoned her own flesh and blood on Christmas Eve, of all times. What kind of circumstances must she be under to prompt her to such an action?"

Heather bit the inside of her lip until she tasted copper. She could easily imagine such a situation—any number of them, actually.

"I agree," Shawn said in a low whisper so as not to startle the baby. "I was thinking the same thing. It's awful even to consider."

"It's the infant we need to worry about right now," Heather stated, her tone threaded with pain. "That's what the mother would have wanted." She believed the baby's mother had taken this drastic step for the sake of her child, and her heart flooded with compassion for both. She could do no less for the unknown woman than to make sure her baby was safe and well cared for.

Shawn's eyes slid to her, then shifted back to the infant. His gaze softened as he stared down at the tiny bundle. "Yes, of course."

Heather rummaged through the box of supplies and produced a bottle of formula she'd mixed together before leaving the house. While she didn't have any infants in her care currently, she'd never managed to get off the formula-makers' sample lists, and she was now glad of it, for the expiration date had not yet passed. "Getting her changed and fed is a good first step, but it's not going to solve the real problem."

Shawn brushed his palm over his jaw, which was taut with strain. "Right. We need to call in the appropriate authorities and decide what needs to happen next. I'll phone the police station first, and then we'd probably better get Delia Bowden on the line to make sure the poor little thing doesn't have any pressing medical problems."

He scoffed and shook his head. "What a mess. I really hate having to disturb everyone in the middle of the night, especially on Christmas Eve."

"It can't be helped, dear," Jo reminded him. "I don't think it's anything we can wait on. The police will probably want to start looking for the baby's mother sooner rather than later. She hasn't had that long to have gotten out of town. We don't know anything about her circumstances—she might be injured. And while she looks fine to me, we can't assume sweet Baby Girl here is healthy until Dr. Delia has had the opportunity to look her over."

Shawn's gaze narrowed and his lips tightened

into a straight line. "If you ladies will stay with the baby, I'll make the calls."

He stepped out of the sanctuary, and Jo slid into the pew next to Heather, holding her arms out for the baby. Heather gently transferred the fragile bundle into the older woman's arms.

"What's your take on all this?" Jo murmured.

Heather shivered, masking it as a shrug. "I can't begin to guess. I feel in my gut that something truly terrible must have happened. It's got to be just horrible for the mother, whoever she is. *Wherever* she is."

"When Shawn returns we should all say a prayer for her," Jo stated with a firm nod that sent her red curls bouncing.

"Mmm." Heather acknowledged Jo's suggestion without agreeing to it. Jo Spencer was a woman of faith, and they were in a church, after all, so Heather supposed it only made sense that prayer would be part of the equation. It wasn't that she had anything against prayer, per se, but it seemed to her like an exercise in futility. Her prayers—not that she'd said many of them lately—seemed as if they bounced off the ceiling and came right back at her. They were certainly never answered.

"I know the police will want to look for her, but I have a feeling she's not of a mind to be found. Chances are she's out of Serendipity by now, though she couldn't have gotten far. Or possibly she's in hiding."

Shawn approached, sliding his cell phone into the chest pocket of his shirt. Heather didn't know how long he'd been listening, but he'd clearly caught Jo's last statement, at the very least. "Can either of you hazard a guess as to who the mother might be? I'm fairly certain it's no one here at the parish."

Heather shook her head. She'd only been back in Serendipity for a few months, and the truth was, she hadn't been overly social during that time. She preferred to spend all her time taking care of her three foster children, attending the older boy's sports games, mentoring her little girl's second-grade class in reading and volunteering for the preschool library day with little Henry. She'd crossed paths with some old friends at the grocery store or the gas station, but she made sure the chats were brief, and any plans to "get together and catch up" were kept deliberately vague. Frankly, she didn't have much time or use for adult company.

She glanced at Jo for the answer to Shawn's question, expecting that she would know something, but to her surprise, the older woman was likewise shaking her head.

"It's the strangest thing," Jo conceded. "I'm not aware of any women in the area who are bursting at the seams to be delivering a precious little bundle of joy—inside or outside the parish."

"So probably not a local, then." Shawn crouched before Jo and wiggled his fingers in front of the baby. The infant grasped his forefinger and pulled it toward her mouth. "She's a strong little thing. A real fighter."

"From the looks of things, she's going to have to be," Jo responded soberly. Both Shawn and Heather agreed with a nod.

Heather's heart physically ached for the baby girl. So sweet. So helpless. The world was harsh even to the tiniest and most innocent of God's creatures.

It wasn't fair. It wasn't *right*.

"So what's next?" Heather asked, clasping her hands in her lap. She wanted to scream and rail at the air with her fists, but she knew that wouldn't serve any purpose. It wouldn't make her feel better in the long run, and it certainly wouldn't help the baby.

"I just got off the phone with Captain James. He's sending Slade and Brody over to meet with us and give us their take on the situation. They should be here any minute now. Oh, and Delia is on her way, as well. She'll be able to give us a better idea if Baby Girl here needs special medical attention."

They didn't have long to wait—one of the blessings of living in a small town. Less than five minutes later, police officers Brody Beckett and Slade McKenna arrived in rumpled uniforms and with sleep-tousled hair. Though they were similar in build, both with the muscular stature of weekend bull riders, Brody was as blond as Slade was dark. Yet their half-asleep expressions matched perfectly. The police station in Serendipity on Christmas Eve was minimally staffed, and Heather guessed the two men were on-call rather than on duty and had been wakened to take this request.

Delia arrived immediately on their heels and went right to work on the baby, fussing over the infant while she checked her with her stethoscope, took her temperature, got her weight with the infant scale she'd brought and looked at her eyes and ears.

"My guess is that she's about three days old," Delia said, looping her stethoscope around her neck. "Eighteen inches and six and a half pounds. Someone's taken adequate care of her and she's not malnourished, although we'll need to keep a close eye on her weight to make sure she doesn't lose any more."

"Did the mother leave anything else behind?" Slade asked, directing his question to Shawn.

"A note, maybe? Something that might clue us in as to why she left her baby in a church?"

Shawn frowned. "I don't think so, other than that tattered Cowboys blanket I found her wrapped in." He gestured toward the altar. "She was in the manger, all alone. It completely freaked me out. I'm sorry. It didn't even occur to me to look around. All I could think about was what I was going to do with the baby."

"That's understandable, and probably just as well," Brody assured him as he and Slade moved toward the crèche. "It may be better that the area was untouched until we got here to investigate."

"Are you considering this to be a crime scene?" Heather asked, shock skittering through her. How could they even think such a thing? Anger welled in her chest. The mother of this baby, whoever she was, needed someone's compassion and assistance, not condemnation and a jail sentence.

Slade glanced her direction. "No. Not yet, anyway, though it's always a possibility. Abandoning a child is a felony in the state of Texas. But we're reserving judgment until we can piece together what really happened here."

"What about safe-haven laws?" Jo asked. "Isn't there anything in the law to protect the mother if it turns out that she can't keep her child?"

"Technically, Serendipity doesn't have an official drop site for a safe haven," Brody explained, his jaw tightening. "We're just too small. We don't have a hospital. An argument could be made that the fire station might be considered an alternative, but even that's kind of iffy."

"Add to that the fact that the mother might not have known what the laws were, or she may not have been in a reasonable state of mind to be able to sort all that out," Heather pointed out, feeling a need to champion the unknown woman. Delia had been holding the infant, but now Heather reached for her, coveting the comforting feeling of the baby in her arms. "She could have been thinking only of the baby's safety. We don't know what circumstances she's facing. Maybe she's poor and can't feed the little darling. Maybe she was being chased by someone. Or she could be in an abusive relationship."

Heather's throat tightened around the words and her stomach lurched at the thought. She struggled for a breath as drops of cold sweat broke out on her forehead.

"Any of that could be true," Slade agreed. "Then again, she could be a hopped-up crackhead who doesn't even care that she's dumped her baby into a stranger's hands."

"At a church," Shawn reminded him gravely.

"The mother left her child at a church. Surely that tells us something—it suggests the woman was cognizant of her baby's needs, that she wanted the best for her. She could have abandoned the baby anywhere. I've heard horrible stories of babies left in Dumpsters or parking lots. That's not what happened in this case. The fact that the mother chose to leave the child here—on Christmas Eve, no less—must mean that she was appealing to our Christian duty to step in and help. Right?"

Heather was surprised to receive help from that quarter. Pastor Shawn was sticking up for the absent mother?

"We shouldn't speculate until we've gathered the facts," Slade conceded. "We don't know what we're dealing with."

"I think I've found something." All eyes turned to Brody, who was crouched next to the manger, sifting through the straw. He withdrew his gloved hand to present a small bundle tied with a dirty red strip of cloth, a seam that looked as if it had been ripped from the bottom of a cotton shirt.

"What is it?" Jo asked as they gathered around.

Brody shifted from a crouch to his knees and set the small bundle on the floor in front of him.

Gingerly, he worked the knot in the cloth until it loosened.

"There's a bit of cash here," Slade said, sifting the contents. "And a crumpled piece of paper. Maybe it's a note?" He dropped it into an evidence bag.

"Can you use fingerprints from the letter to identify the woman?" Shawn asked, moving closer to Slade.

"It's a possibility, but not a great one. If the mom has a criminal record—maybe."

The men appeared to be more interested in the money as Brody rifled through the bills. Heather's attention was on the scrap of paper within the clear plastic evidence bag Jo plucked away from Slade. Heather, Delia and Jo all hovered over the mysterious missive.

"What does it say?" Heather asked, scooting closer to Jo as the older woman carefully handled the evidence bag. Heather's breath caught and held when she laid eyes on the delicate handwriting within the letter. The loops and curls were carefully formed and ornamented, so much so that Heather had the distinct, immediate impression of youth.

"I think we may be dealing with a teen mom," she speculated aloud.

Jo met her gaze, her eyes warm with a mixture of compassion and sorrow. "Unfortunately,

I think you might be right, dear. Though for the life of me I still can't place any woman in Serendipity who looked to be in the family way, most especially a *young* lady. Teenage girls these days keep themselves so blooming skinny. I feel sure I would have noticed if one of them had been expecting."

Heather laid a reassuring hand on Jo's arm. From the tone of the older woman's voice, Heather could tell Jo was taking a good deal of the responsibility for the abandoned baby upon herself. The townspeople often joked that Jo was the first to know everybody's business. In this case, she was clearly calling herself to task for *not* knowing, likely believing that she could have helped the mother if she'd been attentive enough to spot the situation in time. Heather saw no reason for Jo to take any of the blame.

"It may very well be that you don't know her at all. It seems to me that, given the circumstances, it's far more likely that the mother wasn't a local."

"Serendipity is hardly the kind of place one just passes through, especially a teenage girl on her own. And on Christmas Eve, no less. This town is miles away from anywhere significant."

"If she is a stranger, somebody here is bound to have seen her. Or maybe there's a clue in the note."

Jo nodded and held up the missive, adjusting the range to support the farsightedness that came with age. "Wish I had my reading glasses with me," she mumbled, then cleared her throat and began reading aloud. "'Please take care of my baby. She is not safe with me. Her father must never find out I had her. This money is all I have to give.'"

The note was not signed, but there was a hastily scribbled postscript at the bottom of the letter that caught Heather's attention. "'P.S. Her name is Noelle.'"

The men approached just in time to hear the baby's name. Shawn smiled and reached out to brush the palm of his hand over the baby's silky black hair. "It's beautiful. A Christmas name for a Christmas baby."

Heather stiffened. Shawn was close enough that she could smell his spicy aftershave, and though he didn't actually touch her, she knew his palm fell just short of the small of her back as he leaned over to murmur nonsense syllables to Noelle.

"Any clues as to the mother's identity or whereabouts in the note?" Brody asked, leaning forward to see for himself.

Jo shook her head and handed the evidence back to the officer. "Nothing definitive. Heather and I are guessing she's a young mother and not local."

"It sounds like she is running away from the baby's father," Heather added, then hesitated. That wasn't quite right. She, of all people, knew how difficult it was to break free from an abuser's hold on her life. "Or maybe she's staying with him and she's just trying to protect the baby from him," she amended hastily.

"In any case, she's made it perfectly clear that she's not coming back for little Noelle, at least not at present. I think we can work off the assumption that she's gone." Slade frowned, his brow creasing.

Heather was glad that baby Noelle had so many people here concerned about her future, folks who Heather knew would help this child get a running start at life. That was more than many others had.

"There's roughly thirty-five dollars here, mostly ones," Slade informed them, holding out the crumpled wad of cash. "It's not going to get the child very far."

Heather sniffed as tears burned in her eyes. The sound evidently caught Shawn's attention, for he laid a gentle hand on her shoulder and his compassionate blue eyes flashed to hers. Their gazes locked for a moment and he seemed to be probing her thoughts and measuring her feelings, all without speaking a word. She shuddered and physically jerked from him, refusing to be taken in by whatever kindness he was showing her.

This wasn't the time to think of herself, or about Shawn. The baby needed all of their attention. "I believe that was all that the mother had to give."

Chapter Two

All that the mother had to give.

Shawn acknowledged that Heather was probably correct, and his chest squeezed with sympathy. He anxiously wondered where the mysterious young mother was and what she must have been feeling to leave her precious baby in the care of strangers.

He would make this right. He had to. Although he couldn't fathom a reason for it, God must have His reasons for depositing the baby into Shawn's care. He could do no less than follow this thing through to the end. It didn't matter that he had no training in infant care or that he hardly even knew which end of a bottle was up. God willing, he'd figure it out.

He'd been having a running conversation with God ever since the moment he'd first seen the small movement in the hay, and he wasn't about to stop praying now, not when he was facing the possibility of walking a tightrope with no safety net underneath him.

"So the question remains," he said, knowing even before he asked that he was committing himself to something far beyond his scope of expertise. "What are we going to do with an abandoned baby on Christmas Eve?"

"I suppose one of us could drive her into San Antonio, if we can rustle up an infant car seat somewhere," suggested Brody, although with the catch in his voice, he didn't sound particularly warm to the idea.

"And do what with her once you get there?"

Shawn thought he detected an edge of panic in Heather's voice and discreetly narrowed his eyes on her.

Yes, there it was. The flare in the black irises of her eyes, which were surrounded by a beautiful hazel color. She was afraid for this baby. So was Shawn. They all were. Every person in the room knew what taking Noelle to San Antonio in the middle of the night on a holiday would mean—dropping her into the inhospitable hands of an aloof system where she would have no one to be her personal advocate.

But Noelle *had* an advocate. Shawn.

"Do we have a legal obligation to make a permanent decision about her situation tonight?"

Shawn piped up. Maybe with a little time they could figure out a better plan.

Slade raised his dark eyebrows. "Well, eventually we'll have to report her to the proper authorities. Texas social services will want to know about her. But that does not necessarily have to happen tonight. If I'm not mistaken, we have somewhere around one business day to bring her to the attention of the state. The fact that it's Christmas Eve works in our favor, if you're wanting to hold off a bit. *Is* that what you want? And if you don't mind my asking, why? What do you have in mind?"

"Yes, dear," Jo urged, patting Shawn's forearm. "Tell us—what's your plan?"

"I'm not— That is, I don't have a plan. I just can't help but feel this baby was sent to us, to our town, to this church."

To me. He wasn't about to say those words out loud, but he was certainly thinking about them.

"I agree," said Jo. "We know our good Lord. He doesn't make mistakes. Somehow this baby is part of His good and perfect gift to us."

"Amen to that," Delia agreed, adjusting the stethoscope draped around her neck.

Shawn's heart welled even as his stomach tightened. Jo had the extraordinary ability to see the good in everything and everyone, along with the uncanny ability to be able to remind others of God's hand in their life circumstances.

But how could an abandoned baby be a gift from God?

Shawn acknowledged in his heart that the Lord could turn even the worst of circumstances into blessings, but he was struggling to wrap his mind around it. Whatever God had planned for them and for this child, it was beyond his ability to see.

"If we're not going to take Noelle to San Antonio tonight," Slade said, his even tone indicating the statement was a fact and not so much a question, "then what are we going to do with her?"

Shawn took a deep breath and stepped out onto the wire, knowing there was no net below him. If he looked down he knew he would take a mental nosedive, so instead he stared into the stormy blue-eyed gaze of baby Noelle.

"I'll take care of her."

Shawn taking baby Noelle overnight sounded like a reasonable enough plan, at least until four o'clock in the morning came and went and he hadn't gotten a single moment of sleep. The small gathering of neighbors had loaded him up with suggestions on baby care, wished him well and then gone home to catch a few hours of shut-eye before Christmas morning dawned, where they would celebrate with their own families.

Shawn had mistakenly thought he had everything under control. How hard could it be, really?

Ha! The joke was on him. The Lord certainly had a sense of humor.

He groaned and smothered a yawn. Instead of enjoying a happy snooze with sugarplums dancing in his head as he would have done if he'd gone home alone, he was pacing the hallway with an unappeasably fussy baby.

Holding her close to his heart, he gently patted her back in a slow, steady rhythm. The little *bundle of joy* wasn't the least bit happy, and he hadn't a clue what to do for her. He wished he knew what was wrong so he could fix the problem.

After a bottle of formula and a diaper change, Noelle had initially drifted off to sleep. Shawn had thrown together a makeshift bassinet from a shallow plastic bin and some blankets and placed it by the side of his own bed. All was calm—and bright.

For about five seconds.

No sooner had he laid his head on the pillow than Noelle started to wail. And wow, but the kid had a pair of lungs.

He shuffled through his mental list. Diaper changed. Warm bottle. Patting her back to help her remove any lingering bubbles in her tummy. Swaddled. Multiple attempts at a pacifier, although he'd qualified that as a fail, since he couldn't even get the baby girl to keep it in her mouth.

Nothing seemed to work. If anything, the more attention he paid to Noelle, the harder she cried, and now she was making little *hic* sounds when she breathed. He was afraid she was hyperventilating.

Could babies hyperventilate? It frightened him that he didn't even know the answer to that question.

What if she passed out? What if something was seriously the matter with her? Had Dr. Delia missed something critical when she'd examined the baby?

Noelle scrunched up her tiny face and sneezed. Shawn reached for his cell phone, then stopped and shook his head, laughing at how easily flustered he was getting.

Who was he going to call? Emergency services? And say what?

Hello, can you help me? My baby just sneezed!

"I'm overreacting, aren't I, little darlin'?" he murmured to Noelle. Her face relaxed, and she quieted, appearing to respond to the sound of his voice. Well, that was good, right? He kept talking. "Let me tell you, sweetheart, I have a brand-new appreciation for the parents of infants. Is this what Eli and Mary are going through every night right now? Huh? You think?"

Noelle sneezed again.

"Uh-oh. I hope you're not getting sick. Dr. Delia was pretty thorough when she was examining you, and she pronounced you good to go, at least for the time being. But I suppose there's always the possibility that she missed something. Are you coming down with a cold, little darlin'? Or am I just being a worrywart?"

He chuckled softly when he realized Noelle had stopped crying. When he gazed down at her, he realized she was looking at him expectantly, sucking contentedly on her tiny fist.

"So that was all you needed? A little man-to-baby conversation? Well, I don't mind talking to you, sweetheart, but wouldn't it be great if we could table this discussion for now and pick it up in the morning?" From the expectant look on her face, it seemed the answer to that question was no.

Well, if all he had to do was talk, he supposed he could handle that. He was a preacher, after all. Words were his livelihood.

Just not in the middle of the night.

He took a seat on his plush easy chair and kicked back the footrest so he could settle Noelle on his shoulder. He'd heard young parents joking about how their babies had their days and nights mixed up, but he'd never quite understood what that meant.

Now he got it, and got it good.

If nothing else, taking care of Noelle over the Christmas holiday would be a tremendous learning experience for him. After what he'd experienced tonight, he had all kinds of ideas on how to be a better pastor to the parents of newborns in his congregation. Up until this point he realized he'd kind of missed the mark. For one thing, he'd be more sympathetic, and he'd be sure to look for ways to make the transition into parenthood easier. He'd never envisioned the type of sacrifice parents made on a daily—and nightly—basis, and he imagined a strong support system would make all the difference in the world for them.

Noelle gurgled, and Shawn rubbed his fingertips against her tiny back. "What are you here to teach me?" he murmured, offering his heart to God and to the child. "I'm your student now. You've got me in the palm of your sweet little

hand. So why don't you tell me, young lady—
what am I here to learn?"

In a more innocent time of her life, Heather's
favorite time of the year had been Christmas.
Peace on earth, goodwill to all. She recalled
participating in joyful caroling parties with hot
apple cider and eggnog afterward. Joining in the
throng of busy shoppers as they scurried around
trying to catch seasonal deals for their loved
ones. The anticipation as she wrapped presents
and created pretty, elaborate homemade bows
to tie around them. And most of all, she remembered the joy of celebrating God made Man in
the person of Jesus. The nativity.

All of that had been part of her best childhood memories.

But her parents had passed on, and all the
goodness associated with the season had gone
by the wayside during her years with Adrian.
Oh, they'd attended their fair share of Christmas
parties, but Adrian was in the habit of secretly
imbibing on the side. Then afterward, he'd cross
town to where no one knew him and hit the bars
until he was stumbling drunk.

He despised Christmas, and he'd mocked her
attempts to give their house a personal touch
for the season. He'd insisted on professional
decorators and expensive ornaments, and even-

tually she'd just stopped trying. She hadn't even bothered to give any input—it wasn't like anyone listened to her wishes, anyway. It was just more work for her to do and there was no one but her to enjoy it. There wasn't much joy in her life to celebrate. Adrian would complain about the twinkling lights and the space it took up and failed to appreciate the tree and Christmas decor for what they represented.

Church services became exercises in deception. So many people loved and respected Adrian, an active leader and deacon in the church. To members of the congregation, she strived to appear to be the happy, faithful wife of a charming man, with a seemingly perfect marriage and not a care in the world.

What a lie. A whole pack of them, as a matter of fact.

Well, no more.

But even though she no longer carried the weight of the lies on her shoulders, the damage they had done to her still remained. Some days it was all she could do to rise out of bed and go about her daily activities. Her foster children— nine-year-old Jacob, seven-year-old Missy and three-year-old Henry—gave her the strength to face life again. Their precious hugs and sweet laughter made even the worst of days bearable.

This year she'd purchased a freshly cut Virginia pine tree from a tree farm. No artificial trees in her house. If she was being honest, it was as much for her as for the children. It filled her heart with great joy to see the children's excitement as they spotted the perfect tree and hauled it inside. Little hands helped as much as the big ones did.

The tree filled her home with the crisp, refreshing scent of evergreen. She'd helped the kids decorate it with a string of lights and candy canes, and then they'd threaded popcorn and cranberries and draped them over the branches for the final touch. Every cent she made from the state for fostering went straight back into caring for the children, and on the tiny salary she made as a virtual assistant, she was barely making ends meet. It was unfortunate that her finances didn't stretch nearly as far as she would have liked, and this year, at least, she wasn't able to afford the shiny new glass ornaments displayed in the window of Emerson's Hardware, but if her years with Adrian had taught her anything, it was that fancy decorations didn't make for a better holiday.

Simple pleasures were worth treasuring. She was surviving and taking care of the children, and for now, that was enough. She'd budgeted every spare dime to purchase at least one gift for each of the kids from their wish lists, and it was important to her that she followed another old Lewis tradition, so their stockings were overflowing with tokens of her affection, small and inexpensive though they were.

The scene this Christmas morning was picture-perfect. All that was missing was the pitter-patter of feet and the happy squeal of children.

She didn't have to wait long before she heard stirring from down the hall. She promptly attuned her practiced ear to the sound. Muffled whispers emanated from the shadowed spot where the hall met the living room.

"Come out, come out, wherever you are," she called, infusing gaiety into her voice. "Who wants to see what Santa brought this year?"

Heather closed her eyes for a moment and simply savored the lovely sounds of Christmas. Children. Laughing, happy, excited little voices. She allowed the cheerful clatter to penetrate and fill her empty heart and warm her icy spirit.

Her eyes snapped open and her pulse quickened at the sudden shrill buzz of her cell phone. She'd turned the sound back on as she did every morning, but she wasn't expecting a phone call, especially at this time of the morning and on Christmas Day.

She put a hand to her chest to still her galloping heart. She was sick and tired of her first reaction to the phone or doorbell being a spike of terror. It had been several years now since Adrian had been incarcerated, and still she dealt with this. She'd thought moving back home would help. How long would it take her to re-learn the basics, replacing her automatic fear impulses with healthy responses?

"Wait for me, my sweethearts. Don't go looking in your stockings until I'm off the phone," she admonished the children playfully. She reached for the phone in the pocket of her bathrobe. It was a long-standing habit of hers to keep her cell close by, even while she was sleeping. Better safe than sorry.

She glanced at the number. She didn't recognize it, but it was local.

"Hello?" She hoped her voice didn't sound as shaky as she felt.

"Heather? This is Pastor Shawn O'Riley. I apologize for interrupting you on your Christmas morning."

"Shawn?" *The baby.* Heather's adrenaline spiked along with her anxiety. "Is something wrong with Noelle?"

"No—no," he answered hastily. "Well, maybe. I'm not sure. I think perhaps it's just that I don't know what I'm doing. I've never been in charge of a baby before."

Heather pinched her lips and shook her head at the irony. A pastor, a man used to directing others, had in one single night discovered that caring for an infant offered a completely different set of challenges. Even a natural leader couldn't make a baby do what he wanted her to do.

But there were some men who would try.

She shoved out a breath. Shawn had given her no reason to suspect he might fall into that category. "Can you be more specific?"

"Let's see…I've changed her diaper, fed her, burped her—repeatedly, as a matter of fact. It's a never-ending cycle, it seems."

Welcome to parenthood, Heather thought. She'd never had children of her own, but for a while just after graduating from college she'd found great happiness working in a day-care center. In her heart of hearts she'd desperately wanted a baby of her own, but the idea of Adrian fathering any children she might bear had left her frightened beyond words at the prospect of conceiving and bringing a child into her terrifying and hopeless world. She hadn't dared to have a child, who'd have been immediately put at risk.

"Sounds like you're doing everything right," she assured Shawn, forcefully shifting her thoughts to the present. To Noelle.

"I hope so, but I sure don't feel like it. She's a little darlin', but I'm beginning to think I've bitten off more than I can chew, so to speak. I've tried everything. I've done bathing, swaddling, attempting to coax her to take a pacifier—which, incidentally, is much more difficult in practice than it looks at first approach."

Heather chuckled. "It takes some getting used to."

"Yes, but here's my problem. The one thing I cannot get her to do is *sleep*. She'll only doze off for a few minutes at a time, and even then, it's only if I'm rocking her in my arms. The moment I try to lay her down on her own, her eyes pop back open and she starts wailing in earnest. Then the whole process begins again." He sighed deeply.

It sounded as if the poor man was sleep-deprived in a major way. Heather imagined it was hard enough to care for a newborn when there were two parents in the house to tag-team on getting some rest. She had to admire Shawn for taking such immense responsibility on his own shoulders, even for one night. It wasn't something she would have expected from a single man.

But why was he calling her?

"Is there something I can help you with?" she asked, her breath catching in her throat as she waited for his answer.

His groan was one of utter defeat. "No. Not

really. I guess I just wanted to hear the sound of someone's voice, an adult someone, that is— and maybe be reassured that I'm doing everything I need to be doing for Noelle. I don't want to mess this up. Jo Spencer considers you the resident expert, since you raise foster kids and have worked in day care and everything. I figured you were the one to call. I would hate to think I accidentally overlooked something important that I could have done to make Noelle more comfortable. Anyway, thanks for listening. I appreciate it."

"Do you have anyone who could come over and spell you for a while so you can get some sleep?" Heather didn't know why she asked. It wasn't as if this situation had anything to do with her. Not directly. She wasn't Shawn's friend, and she didn't want to be, thank you very much. But this concern she felt wasn't truly for his sake, was it? No, it was for Noelle. The sweet baby deserved loving, capable care. And while Shawn seemed to be earnestly trying his best, he was unpracticed at child care even when he *wasn't* sleep-deprived. "A friend? A neighbor?"

"No. This is all on me. I wouldn't want to pull anyone away from sharing Christmas with their families." He stifled a yawn. "I'm sure I'll make it…somehow."

"I can't leave my foster kids."

"Of course not." He sounded genuinely surprised. "I wouldn't expect you to, even if you could."

"My parents are no longer living, so I don't have any help from that quarter." She didn't know why she felt the need to rationalize her actions to him, but there it was. "I'm single. I have no one else to watch them."

"Seriously, Heather. I'm not asking for you to go out of your way for me and Noelle. I guess I shouldn't have called. I didn't mean to bother you or to put any kind of pressure on you."

"You aren't bothering me," she replied, which was half true. It would be a good long time, if ever, before she was completely comfortable around men—particularly those who claimed to be men of faith. But this was about the baby, and making sure the tiny infant was taken care of could never be a bother.

She squeezed her eyes closed and took a deep breath—in through the nose, out through the mouth—as she'd learned through many, many months of therapy.

Be calm. Relaxed. Composed.

She knew she was going to regret the next words coming out of her mouth, but she'd made a promise to herself and God that she'd help children in need whenever and wherever she found them. It was, in a sense, her penance for all of the mistakes she had made.

And at this moment, that meant she was going to help Noelle.

There was nothing she could do for the two children who'd died instantly after being sideswiped by Adrian's car as he swerved all over the road in a drunken haze. She couldn't turn back the clock and keep Adrian from walking out the door on that fateful day, even though she'd known he'd had too much to drink and that he was going to get behind the wheel and drive. She'd only been thinking about herself at the time. She'd wanted him gone, and she'd let him walk away.

She wished she could make things right, but she couldn't. However, she *could* do something for the tiny baby who'd been abandoned by her mother on Christmas Eve. She could—and she would.

"I know I said I can't leave my kids alone in the house, but that doesn't mean you can't come over here. I will set an extra plate, and you and Noelle can join us for Christmas dinner. I'm sure the kids would love to have extra guests at the table. I'll be happy to watch Noelle for a bit while you catch a power nap. Unless you have other plans, that is."

"No. No other plans. But are you sure I won't

be imposing on you?" Relief was evident in his voice.

"No." *Yes.* "Not at all."

"Well, then."

Why was he hesitating? Could he hear the tentativeness in *her* tone?

"Oh, that's right. You don't have a car seat, do you?" She slung out a guess.

"That's not a problem. A car seat isn't necessary. It's not an immediate issue, anyway. I'll have to procure one eventually, I suppose, if I'm going to be the one taking Noelle to the authorities in San Antonio. But today, we can walk."

Her shoulders slumped in relief and she dragged in a silent breath. He hadn't noticed her uncertainty, then. *Good.*

"Then it's settled. I'll set an extra plate for you. Come over whenever you're ready. Oh, and be sure to bundle Noelle up really well. There's a bit of a chill in the air."

"You're sure you don't mind the extra company?"

No, she wasn't sure. She would never be sure. Probably not for one single day for the rest of her life. And she wished he would stop asking, or she was liable to give in to her doubts and capitulate.

"I'm absolutely certain," she reassured him for what she hoped was the last time. "I'm looking forward to seeing that precious little blessing of yours."

At least that was the truth.

Chapter Three

Shawn had never been so uncomfortable in his life. Being the kind and thoughtful woman she was, Heather hadn't said as much out loud, but it didn't take a rocket scientist to figure out that he was intruding on her personal family time—and that she was only allowing it because he was entirely inadequate to the task of caring for an infant.

From the moment he'd stepped into the house, Heather had swept Noelle into her arms and taken over all of the baby care. How quickly she had put the poor little infant's world to rights. Heather had also fixed *his* most pressing problem, insisting he head straight into Jacob's bedroom for a quick nap.

He'd dropped into a dead sleep but had been wakened shortly after by a phone call from Jo, inquiring how he was faring with Noelle. She hadn't even sounded a little bit surprised when he revealed he had come to Heather's house for help. Probably because Jo already suspected how hopeless he'd be with an infant.

Why no one had bothered to inform *him* that he wasn't up to the task was beyond him. No one had uttered a single word of warning. Instead, every last one of them had played right along last night when he'd unwittingly offered to care for the infant. No one had laughed. No one had even seemed startled by his hasty proposal. They'd let him dive right off the side of a cliff without testing the depth of the water first.

How could he have known what he was letting himself in for? He was a simple cowboy preacher. He knew ranching and he had the gift of gab. He was a single man and lived alone. His needs were few.

Noelle's needs were apparently many, or at least they were a mystery to him, and he was clearly lacking in his ability to take decent care of her. At least here with Heather, he could be assured that Noelle would have everything she needed. Though the downside was that he'd have Heather as a witness to see exactly how inept he truly was. He grinned, not bothered by the laughter that was bound to come at his expense—and if there wasn't yet, there soon would be. Christmas Day wasn't over. He had a while yet to display the stunning depths of his incompetence.

He didn't really care if other folks caught a laugh or two over his present circumstances— he was laughing at himself. It was pretty funny, when he thought about it.

Chuckling, Shawn assured Jo that all was well for the time being. It was all good *now*— because of Heather's generosity and help. Jo laughed with him and agreed with his assessment of Heather and then promised she'd check in on him later. Shawn tucked his cell phone into his shirt pocket and stretched to get the kinks out of his shoulders. Now that he was awake, he wasn't sure what he should be doing.

Probably leaving. He didn't want to take advantage of Heather's kindness, particularly on what he understood to be her first Christmas with her foster children.

But when he padded back into the living room and spied Noelle and Heather looking so comfortable and contented together in the rocking chair, he couldn't find it in his heart to break them up. And truth be told, even considering how awkward he felt right now being the third wheel, he wasn't yet prepared to go off on his own and face another night of single-parent foster-daddy duty.

He shuffled toward the corner of the living

room, his hands stuffed into the pockets of his blue jeans. He probably should at least offer to do something to help, but he hadn't the faintest notion of what assistance he could give. He wasn't family. He wasn't technically even a guest. He didn't know where she kept the silverware. His cooking skills were marginal. And though he could probably manage to keep the older kids occupied, he was totally useless with the baby.

"You don't have to hold up the wall," Heather commented with a gentle smile, brushing a long strand of mahogany-brown hair behind her ear. "Feel free to sit wherever you can find a free space, although it looks like you may have to move something to find a seat. I usually have a rule about putting away toys before new ones get taken out, but I'm being a little lax today, since it's Christmas."

He smiled and nodded to acknowledge her offer, but he was too fidgety to sit down just yet. Besides, standing gave him a better view of the kids. There was nothing like the sight and sound of jubilant children on Christmas morning to raise a man's spirits.

Crumpled wads of bright-colored Christmas wrap, now ripped and forgotten, lay balled underneath the glittering tree. Heather's three foster children were busy with their new toys. The boys, nine-year-old Jacob and three-year-old Henry, played together, pushing their shiny cast-model race cars around a plastic track. Seven-year-old Missy held a new doll in the curve of her arm and mimicked Heather's sounds and movements as she held Noelle. It was a heart-warming sight, especially since just yesterday he'd imagined he'd spend the day as a lonely bachelor.

What a difference a day could make. Here he was, enveloped in the warmth of a child-filled house. He hadn't realized just how wonderful it would be after having been alone all these years. It filled his heart with great joy to realize how little it took to make the young ones happy. He needed a little bit more of that innocence in his life. If only adults had the same capacity to give and receive as generously as the youngsters.

Heather hadn't gone overkill on the number or size of the gifts—whether because she couldn't or she chose not to, but there was no shortage in the amount of joy she'd given her children in what they *had* received. It was abundantly clear to anyone observing the scene that she knew each of her foster children intimately and was mindful of what they wanted and needed.

Shawn was envious of that quality in her. *He* apparently hadn't been able to anticipate Noelle's needs at *all*.

It was a good thing for the baby that he wasn't going to end up being her permanent foster parent. She would no doubt go to a wonderful home with a foster mother like Heather, who had the knowledge and capacity to care for her. All of her needs would be anticipated and met without Shawn's doltish stops and starts. She was such a sweet little girl, and he was certain she'd eventually be adopted by a nice Christian family with a mom and a dad who loved each other. Maybe she'd have other siblings to play with and a dog and a cat and a yard with a fence.

All he had to offer was the dog and the cat and the yard and the fence—and pigs and goats and horses and ranch land.

Not good enough. Not by any stretch of the imagination.

He shifted his attention back to Heather, who watched over her brood from an old-fashioned wooden rocking chair laden with colorful floral cushions. She hummed a Christmas carol as she rocked. She had a lovely, rich alto voice that enthralled Shawn as much as it did Noelle, purring through his muscles until he felt thoroughly relaxed and yet completely alert at the same time. It was an odd paradox, but true nonetheless.

To his utter astonishment, he discovered that Noelle, who was contentedly curled in the crook of Heather's arm, wasn't asleep as he'd first assumed she must be. Instead, she was staring up at Heather, her chubby fist in her mouth and her eyes just beginning to focus on the woman holding her.

What she *wasn't* doing was crying. Not wailing, not squalling, not bawling, not even a whimper.

Go figure.

Shawn was amazed by how quickly Heather had made everything right in the tiny baby's world. He didn't know if it was because she was experienced in caring for infants or the fact that she was naturally suited to be a mother. Maybe it was a combination of both, but Noelle responded to Heather in a way that made Shawn feel especially incompetent, a fact which, while impressive, grated against his distinctly male pride. *He* wanted to do it right, get things done the first time and in an expedient manner—not stumble over his every move.

He watched in awe as the baby took a bottle from Heather without a fuss. Adding insult to injury, Noelle fell asleep while Heather was in the midst of patting her back.

Heather definitely must know some tricks of the trade that he didn't. Or maybe the tiny tyke was plain old worn-out from her self-appointed task of keeping Shawn awake all night. She had to sleep sometime, right?

Just not on his watch.

Shawn shifted his weight and smothered a yawn behind his fist. The catnap he'd taken was a drop in the bucket after the past twenty-four hours. It wasn't just the fact that he'd had to stay awake, although there was that. It had been quite a few years since he'd pulled an all-nighter. But there was a great deal more to the fatigue weighing him down—like the stress of being singularly responsible for a tiny human life, completely helpless and dependent upon him.

"You still look thoroughly exhausted," Heather commented. She tilted her chin and blinked up at him with her big hazel eyes that softly glimmered from the lights of the tree. "I think maybe you need to sleep a little bit longer. There's no rush, you know. I don't mind watching the baby this afternoon."

Caught up in her gaze, Shawn's stomach did a little flip and he barely stanched the urge to clear the catch out of his throat.

"Jo woke me when she phoned to check on Noelle. I attempted to go back to sleep but my mind started spinning with all that's been going on and that was the end of my nap. As tired as I am, I don't think I could sleep any more."

"That's a shame. Maybe you should have put your phone on mute." She smiled, though it looked a bit forced. "Well, in any case, you don't have to stand in the corner. You look like a hat stand—or else like someone put you in time-out."

Shawn chuckled. "It wouldn't be the first time."

"And probably not the last. Seriously—please come sit down on the couch and take a load off. You make me nervous when you hover that way." Despite her kidding tone, he almost got the sense that she truly *was* nervous. But that couldn't be right, could it? What reason would she have to be nervous around him?

"I don't even mind if you put your feet up on the coffee table—well, the storage bench that serves as the coffee table—either," she continued. "As far as I'm concerned, that's what it's there for."

"Not for decoration? It's a nice-looking piece of furniture." The bench looked as if it fit with the rest of her decor—not that he was any kind of expert on matters of decorating. The padded corners were a little worn, but it exhibited the same lived-in look as her other furnishings. He liked lived-in.

She chuckled. "No fancy furniture in this household. *Decorative* would last about a day.

With three kids running around, functional is the name of the game here."

He groaned in delight as the plush cushions on the chocolate-colored couch enveloped him like gentle arms. True comfort. Everything about Heather's house suggested it was the genuine article. Her entire home expressed her heart—and it was all about the children.

Her home was far more comfortable and welcoming than the more perfectly kept, sanitized houses of some of his congregants, where he found himself tiptoeing around, afraid to stand near the furniture, much less sit on it. He felt ill at ease in too-clean houses. As a pastor, visiting his flock was one of his favorite tasks, but as a cowboy who lived and worked on a ranch with horses and goats and pigs, he wasn't always dust-and-dirt-free. Heather certainly didn't need to apologize for her furniture. He wished everyone kept a house like hers.

She was literally encouraging him to put his feet up.

Sweet!

All he needed now was a cold soft drink and a football game on television—although of course he'd never suggest such a thing. He'd already probably put enough dents into her holiday without bringing sports into it.

"I can't believe how worn-out I feel," Shawn

said, running a hand across the stubble on his jaw and belatedly realizing he hadn't shaved that morning. Now that he thought about it, he hadn't combed his hair before he left, either— and then he'd gone and taken a nap, which could only have served to worsen his already disheveled appearance. He must look like the abominable snowman's twin brother, and yet Heather hadn't blinked an eye, not when he'd appeared at the door, and not when he'd shuffled out after his nap. "I don't know how new parents do it, but I'm certainly too old to try to pull all-nighters anymore."

Heather raised a brow and huffed a breath through her teeth. "You're not exactly over the hill. What are you—twenty-six? Twenty-seven?"

"Twenty-nine, although at the moment I feel more like I'm sixtysomething. Was it only a few years ago when I was in seminary that I could stay up all night with ease? Seems like forever. Me and my buddies used to get lost in these deep theological debates. They'd last for hours, many times the whole night, and then I would go straight to my classes the next day without so much as a yawn. I studied for finals that way, too. Pulled all-nighters and managed to do well on my tests without much more assistance than a stout cup of coffee or an energy drink to back me up. Now look at me." He chuckled and hung his head with a dramatic groan. "One night with a baby and I'm as good as gone."

She laughed. "It might be the stress that's really taking it out of you, you know. Watching a baby isn't for the weak of heart. I've never been the parent of an infant myself, but I saw plenty of them during my experience as a day-care director. If I don't miss my guess, all new parents go through this no-sleeping stage, at least to some extent. I remember my first few nights as a foster parent of these three sweet-hearts—hovering over the kids' beds when they were sleeping just to check and make sure they were all breathing. I was hypervigilant for the entire first month, I think. And my kids aren't even infants."

Shawn groaned and shoved his fingers through his hair. He appreciated the way Heather was trying to make him feel better, but he still believed he'd epically failed in something that up until last night he'd simply and erroneously assumed was easy. He apparently lacked the entire skill set for being a father. "Thankfully, I'm not a real parent yet. I always thought I'd have a family someday, of course, but now I've got to admit I'm questioning how smart that would be. I'm not sure I can handle this *daddy* business. Unless maybe it's different when it's your own kid."

Heather shrugged and dropped her gaze from his, but he thought he detected sadness in her gaze before she looked away. "I wouldn't know. It might be. Do you regret agreeing to care for Noelle through the holiday?"

Regret? No, that wasn't the word he would use to describe what he was feeling about fostering Noelle.

Heather's soft-spoken question jarred him to the core. Despite the lack of sleep, Shawn's heart went out to baby Noelle in a way he couldn't even explain. He believed God had His hand in placing Noelle in the manger at his little chapel instead of at the police station or firehouse. Sure, he missed the sleep he would have gotten. But the regret would be a hundred times stronger if he hadn't made the choice to take the baby in.

He shook his head. "No. I'm glad for the opportunity. And I do believe God put Noelle into my life for a reason. I won't soon forget her. She's stolen a piece of my heart. If nothing else comes of this, the experience will give me a better pastoral understanding for new parents in my little parish."

Shawn didn't miss the way her jaw ticked when he mentioned God. He had a feeling there was a reason why she didn't attend church, but even though he was curious, now was hardly the time to press her on the issue. She was virtually a stranger to him, and yet she'd opened up her home and her holiday to him, and even more important, to Noelle. She had a good heart and acted on her kindness.

She brushed a kiss across the baby's forehead. "I think you're right about her making a difference in people's lives. She's affected me as well, the little dear. I just hope Noelle's mother finds the help she needs. Whatever circumstances led her to giving up her baby, she has to be hurting right now."

"I've been praying for her nonstop," Shawn agreed. "We may not know where she is, but God does. He can help her in ways we never could."

There was that tic again, only this time Heather narrowed her eyes on him. She was clearly scrutinizing him, but for what? What did she think she was going to see in his gaze?

Suddenly uncomfortable, he started to get to his feet, but Heather beat him to it, covering the distance between them in two steps and sliding Noelle into his arms. "I think she's going to sleep for a while, especially since she was so restless last night. If you can hold the baby and keep an eye on the kiddos for me, I'll go see if

I can get our supper ready. The ham is probably done but I've got some side dishes to finish. In the meantime, let me pull out some appetizers. I've got a veggie snack tray and ranch dip in the refrigerator, or I can put together tortilla chips and some salsa if you'd prefer."

Her queries were coming a mile a minute and though Shawn repeatedly tried to answer her rapid-fire questions, he couldn't get a word in edgewise. She appeared to be trembling—both physically and emotionally. He didn't have a clue what had caused this sudden alteration in her mood. Was it something he'd said?

If Heather was flustered, Shawn was now doubly so. All his pastoral training deserted him in a flash. Something about Heather set him off-kilter in a way visiting with his parishioners and hanging out with his neighbors normally did not.

He shifted Noelle so she rested on his shoulder, careful to keep a hand curled around her neck to give her extra support. Silently he took a mental step backward and scanned his recent conversation with Heather, filtering it for clues as to where he'd gone wrong. Somewhere along the way they'd taken a detour.

His reference to the Almighty was bothering her—of that much he was certain. Beyond that, he couldn't say, although he sensed it was more than just the one thing that had gotten her so upset. He made a mental note to back off speaking about anything religious for now, although he acknowledged that was going to be difficult for him to do.

It wasn't so much that he was a preacher with the deep desire to press his religion on everyone. The only truth he wanted to preach was how he lived his life. That was his faith message, much more so than the words he spoke. His real problem was that since he didn't have a family, his pastorate pretty much summed up his life. Try making nonreligious conversation over that. He didn't even have any notable hobbies to speak of, other than his ranch and the animals he kept, and he doubted the ins and outs of his pig-breeding program would interest her.

He belatedly realized she'd suddenly stopped hammering him with questions and glanced up to see her waiting with an expectant look on her face, one fist propped on the delicate curve of her hip as she waited for his response.

He cleared his throat and stared back up at her. He was absolutely lost. Heat started at the tips of his toes and crept all the way up to his ears. What had she been talking about?

Oh, yeah. Right. Food. Appetizers. Vegetables or chips.

"Either one would be fine," he answered,

stammering over his words. "Whatever works for you works for me. I'm easy. When I was a kid, my mama used to say I'd eat anything as long as it wasn't moving."

She chuckled. "Well, I think I can promise you that."

He swallowed, knowing he needed to acknowledge her teasing, but his amusement had dissipated the moment his mother's face flashed through his mind. Regret stabbed his gut, thinking of his mom—his dad.

And David.

Holidays were especially difficult for him, but he didn't like to dwell on it. He pressed the blackened, charred ruins of his family memories to the back of his thoughts and forced a smile for Heather's sake. "Whatever you and the kids would rather have."

She nodded crisply. "I'll put the vegetable tray out, then. The kids all like the carrot sticks. Would you like me to turn a game on the television while you wait? I'll try not to turn the volume up too much so it doesn't wake Noelle, but I definitely want to hear what's happening, especially with the Texas game. I'm a die-hard Longhorn fan."

"You like college football?"

"Doesn't everyone?" She sounded genuinely

surprised. "I've been a fan since I was knee-high to a grasshopper."

Shawn didn't know why it shocked him to discover that about her, but it did. It wasn't as if Heather was the first woman who'd expressed an interest in football. He'd been to countless Super Bowl parties in mixed company. But Heather's voice held an excited, nearly fanatic died-in-the-wool tone, and he sensed a kindred spirit, college-football wise.

"I'm a Baylor fan, myself."

She wrinkled her nose. "I'll forgive you this once. But only because I'm feeling especially generous, today being Christmas and all."

They shared a laugh. Shawn felt better, and for the briefest moment, the tension in Heather's expression dissolved. He caught a glimpse of the true beauty in the woman, which until that moment had been hidden behind the mask of whatever burdens she silently carried. He didn't know what troubled her, but he knew those burdens were there. His breath caught as her hazel eyes, green irises shadowed with flames of burnt orange, locked with his. Her gaze shifted, turning anxious, and then he saw it all—those things of which she had not spoken.

Love. Loss. Pain.

His throat bobbed as he searched for words of comfort, anything to let her know that he got it. He might not know the details, but he didn't have to know what or who had hurt her to sympathize with her.

But before he could speak, the doorbell rang.

Heather's breath returned with a fevered gasp as the peal of the doorbell severed the magnetic draw of Shawn's gaze. Her adrenaline-shocked pulse hammered relentlessly as waves of panic washed through her. She closed her eyes and concentrated on evening out her breathing. Meanwhile, she fought the anger and resentment that rose to the surface, unwanted and uninvited, knowing stress would only make her reaction more pronounced. Fighting the anger, at the circumstances and at herself, was hard. She hated that she had no control over when and how these episodes occurred. Her panic attacks weren't always rational, nor were they necessarily based entirely on emotion. Sometimes they just appeared out of nowhere, for no good reason whatsoever. She'd been warned it might happen, yet she still couldn't get used to having such strong physical responses she couldn't control.

For the first time in many months, it wasn't initially or even primarily the doorbell that had startled her. She couldn't have been more stunned than she was to find the first thing that popped into her head when she closed her eyes wasn't the nightmare of being chased down by Adrian.

Confusion reigned, and she knew it showed outwardly in the flush of her cheeks. But how could she not be perplexed as she frantically sorted through her feelings? She was absolutely floored to find that among the myriad of emotions she was currently experiencing, fear was surprisingly low on the list.

When Shawn had looked at her, she felt as if he'd really *seen* her—glimpsed into her heart at the woman hiding deep within. That should have scared the socks off of her.

It hadn't. Shawn hadn't frightened her, at least not in the way she'd been accustomed to in the past. He'd thrown her for a loop. She suspected he'd seen more of her than she wanted, and that was cause for panic. But he hadn't frightened her.

What *had* happened? These days, she was always so careful not to let her guard down. Not ever. Most especially not with men. Shawn was a pastor, but that was hardly a recommendation to Heather. It certainly didn't procure any kind of confidence in him. She didn't trust church leaders as far as she could throw them. For all she knew, Shawn was the worst kind of charlatan, profiting off unsuspecting folks in the name of God.

And yet—there was something different about Shawn. There had been no judgment in his gaze, only compassion for whatever he read in her eyes. Not many men in Heather's life had ever bothered to look beyond the shell of her physical appearance. Any outward beauty she possessed was a curse, and the have-it-all-together woman she presented to the world was a counterfeit. She sensed that Shawn had not only seen that which she strove to keep hidden, but had somehow reached out to her and touched her inner person.

That rattled her more than any physical contact ever could.

"Don't move," she snapped a little more harshly than she intended. "You've got the baby. I'll get the door."

Relieved to be away from Shawn's probing gaze, she rushed forward and swung the front door open wide, forgetting even to check through the peephole to see who it might be. That *moment* with Shawn had shaken her up to the point where even her common sense had rocketed out of her reach. She supposed it was also possible that she wasn't as concerned over who was at the door because she was bolstered by Shawn's presence in the house, but she wasn't ready to go down that path, even if it was only in her mind. The last thing she needed or wanted was to be dependent on a man—for anything. And she would certainly never depend on a man to make her feel safe.

Besides, facts were facts. Adrian was in prison, and he was going to be in there for a good long time. She had nothing to fear, though her psyche sometimes forgot that. Maybe she was finally getting used to the truth. Maybe eventually she could put all her fear behind her and move on with her life.

"Merry Christmas, my dears," Jo Spencer exclaimed the moment the door was opened. The stout redhead stepped inside the foyer without waiting to be invited. Her arms were laden with parcels—a plate of cookies and several festive gift bags.

"Comin' through," shouted a scratchy voice from behind Jo as her husband, Frank, entered the house. "Jo brought me along to be her packhorse," he grumbled. "Where do you want all this stuff?"

Like Jo, Frank had his arms full, mostly of canvas bags with the Sam's Grocery logo on it, filled with what seemed to be baked goods and baby clothes.

"Head straight back to the kitchen, Frank," Heather instructed with a chuckle. She didn't take the least bit of offense to Frank's curtness. Few in Serendipity did. He was a lovable old man for all his guff. "I haven't set up the table for the meal yet, so you can place all your parcels there."

"Chance and Phoebe told us to make sure to wish y'all a happy Christmas, as well," Jo continued, ignoring her husband's griping. "Naturally all the stores around here are closed for the holiday, so we've got nothing new to offer you, but Phoebe dug through a few boxes of their baby things and managed to find a few pieces to help clothe Noelle. Nothing pink, I'm afraid, seeing as their youngest is a boy, but they found a few one-pieces and such in green and yellow that I think will do nicely."

Heather's heart welled, as did the tears in her eyes. Her throat constricted, and she found herself at a loss for words.

Her nerves snapped to attention when Shawn's voice came from directly behind her. "That's very kind of y'all to think of us on Christmas day, and especially to go out of your way to help out baby Noelle."

"Nothing exceptionally out-of-the-ordinarily kind about being neighborly," Jo said, bustling around the table, removing a couple of glass casserole dishes and a cherry pie from the pile of bags. "Did you remember to grab the whipped cream, Frank?"

The old man snorted. "What do you think? You only reminded me about it three times before we left."

"So in other words you're tellin' me you forgot it, then?" Jo chuckled and bussed Frank's scruffy cheek.

"No, old woman, I'm tellin' you that you're a nag." He reached into one of the canvas bags and withdrew a large tub of whipped topping, then tossed it to Shawn without warning.

Heather was impressed by Shawn's quick reflexes. He caught the bucket easily with just one hand and with a single smooth move deposited it into the freezer.

"You see there, son?" Frank continued, wrapping an affectionate arm around Jo's ample waist. "You'd better be a hundred and ten percent certain before you go and tie the knot, 'cause this is what you'll have to put up with."

The words were as grumpy as usual. If Heather had been going only by those, she would no doubt have found herself smack-dab in the middle of another panic attack. But it wasn't about the words. It was the looks the couple shared between them. The actions and affection that set them apart. Frank and Jo Spencer exemplified what Heather had once believed marriage could be. Love conquers all. It didn't matter how different Frank and Jo were from each other—and they were about as different from each other as two people could be. But it was perfectly obvious to Heather, and no doubt to everyone else who had ever met the old couple, that love bridged that gap.

She didn't know how they did it. Whatever their secret, it was clearly beyond her understanding. She'd made every mistake a woman could make, one right after the other, leading not only to heartbreak, but the death of innocent children.

Heather blinked against the burning sensation in her eyes and turned her gaze away, fighting to breathe around the lump of emotion in her throat. She couldn't stand it. She really couldn't stand it.

Even in the face of kindness, why did life have to be so hard?

Chapter Four

Shawn leaned over the sink to splash his face free of shaving cream, careful not to drip water onto the little bundle of joy strapped to his chest by a baby carrier. He hummed as he dried his jaw with a hand towel, partially because Noelle seemed to appreciate either his voice or the vibration of his chest, and partially out of sheer gratitude as he remembered the outpouring of love and generosity parishioners had given him—*them*—on Christmas Day. Even though he'd been the pastor of his small congregation for several years, remembering the incredible scene at Heather's house still sent him reeling with thankfulness for so many blessings.

Good people. Wonderful, amazing friends and neighbors.

After Jo and Frank had come and gone, he and Heather had been visited by at least a dozen other families, all bringing supplies for Noelle and extra food and gifts for Heather and her kids. He knew he shouldn't be stunned at how quickly the word got around town that there was a baby in need, nor the amazing way people responded when they heard.

Serendipity was like that. Folks cared for each other, even to the point of interrupting their own holidays to make sure little Noelle had what she needed. Of course it wasn't enough that everyone had had such open hearts toward the baby. They'd been thinking of Heather and her children as well, which Shawn considered far more than merely the icing on the cake. He had a whole new appreciation for living in Serendipity.

Since Christmas Day was on a Friday, Shawn had been able to spend the whole weekend with Noelle, and he was glad for the opportunity. His sleep deprivation hadn't lessened, but that was to be expected. He was proud of how well he'd managed to adjust to the role of foster father. Of course, it helped knowing Heather was no more than a phone call away. He experienced far less pressure with Heather as his right-hand woman, and he had, in fact, made use of her expertise several times over the past two days.

There was definitely a steep learning curve where infants were concerned, at least for him.

Someone had slipped him a copy of a baby-care book in one of the bags, which probably would have been a tremendous help to him—*if* he'd had nine months to prepare and memorize every line in the manual. It wasn't as if he had time to sit down and read *any* book cover to cover between feeding and diapering duty, and yet that was probably exactly what he needed to do. Somehow. In his nonexistent spare time. As it was, he was grateful for the index and the table of contents that allowed him to turn to specific pages for assistance.

But as nice as the book was, it was nothing close to the advantage of having Heather on his side. She was infinitely patient with him, and didn't seem to mind his endless string of clueless and sometimes brainless questions, nor the fact that he phoned her quite literally every couple of hours, even in the middle of the night. She'd been a great deal more than a shoulder to lean on. She was practically holding him up. She'd offered to spell him again if he needed her to take the baby for a while and gracefully let him know he could avail himself of the charity of her home should he need a bit more shut-eye than he was getting on his own.

He'd considered her invitation and more than once had been on the brink of accepting it, but thankfully, he and Noelle seemed to be hitting a stride with each other and he hadn't had to put Heather out any more than he already had. He was certainly bothering her enough just with the numerous phone calls and questions. No need to further complicate matters by becoming a mainstay at her house.

She already had her three kids to take care of. She didn't need two more.

Now that it was Monday, they'd made plans to take Noelle to San Antonio to meet with the social worker who was the point person for Heather and her three children. Heather had arranged for a neighbor to take care of Jacob, Missy and Henry so she could accompany him, giving him even more reason to be grateful for her. He was racking up quite a bill of kindnesses given to him, and he knew he'd never be able to repay her. Not only was she encouraging him by her presence and her connections, but she'd even offered to drive him to town. He was glad she was going along, if nothing else, to remind him of what a really good foster parent looked like—and to underscore the fact that he wasn't that person.

With every minute that ticked closer to their appointment time, he found himself more urgently needing the reminder that he was *not* the right person to see to Noelle's care on any kind of permanent basis. And what kind of crazy was that for him to even consider? Noelle deserved better than a cowboy pastor with zero parenting experience.

He would have thought that as much as he'd struggled to care for Noelle, especially at the beginning, he'd be anxious to put her into decent care with people who knew what they were doing. So why was this so hard? It shouldn't be, practically speaking, but his heart wasn't listening. It was going to be difficult for him to hand her off to a stranger.

Painful.

Maybe it was his lack of sleep, or maybe it was that he'd had two days with no one to talk to except Heather and the tiny infant, but he had bonded with Noelle. It was the strangest thing. He felt as if his large heart was tied to her tiny one by a delicate thread—a string that would snap the moment Noelle was lifted from his arms.

If he had a wife by his side to mother the infant, he knew he wouldn't think twice before volunteering to foster Noelle, maybe even adopt her. But he didn't. And even with a woman by his side, he wasn't sure he'd ever be father material.

His own family was a train wreck of gigantic proportions. Shawn acknowledged that he was the cause of all his family's ills. A mother hospitalized under permanent psychiatric care. A father who loved the bottle more than his life. His brother…

He couldn't let himself think about David.

There was no way he could ever put another human being in that kind of jeopardy. He didn't trust himself, and never would. As much as his heart went out to Noelle, he couldn't be responsible for a child's life.

He brushed a blue terry-cloth towel down his face to remove traces of aftershave and stared at himself in the mirror, but he didn't see his own reflection. Instead, he saw his younger brother's face.

Little six-year-old David, his ginger hair sticking to his sweaty forehead, his fair, freckled skin burned and red. His palms flat against the surface of the car window, fingers spread. His mouth open wide in a silent scream, pleading for Shawn to reach him.

To save him.

Shawn shuddered and turned away from the mirror. He hadn't been able to rescue David, and he hadn't been able to salvage what was left of his mother's sanity after her younger son had died. His father had never picked up a drink in his life until he'd watched his younger son being lowered into the ground.

Shawn had done that. He had failed his family on every conceivable level.

Noelle needed better than that. She needed safety. Security. Someone who knew what he or she was doing, someone confident around an infant and able to make the kind of permanent commitment the baby required.

She needed a good family who would give her the love and care she deserved.

Please, God, let it be so.

His prayer was shortened by the sound of a car horn.

Heather.

Shawn didn't want to keep her waiting. He grabbed the infant car seat off the kitchen table on his way out, thankful that Zach and Delia had been willing and able to temporarily loan it to him for Noelle's one-way trip into San Antonio. He swallowed back the emotion that burned his throat. There was no point in his buying a car seat for her when he'd only need it for today. Her new foster parents would no doubt purchase one for her.

Ignoring the ache in his chest, he exited the house and waved to Heather as he approached her silver midsize SUV. She hurried around to the passenger side and opened the back door while he unfastened Noelle from the baby carrier on his chest.

Yuletide Baby

"The car seat goes in the middle," she informed him, gesturing toward the interior. "Why don't you let me hold the baby while you get it snapped in?"

He nodded and handed Noelle to Heather, giving his shoulders a mental straightening as he turned to meet this new challenge—strapping in a car seat. It couldn't possibly be that difficult, right? Besides, he'd looked up the directions online, although he probably wouldn't admit that part aloud. It was a first for him, but he didn't want to look incompetent around Heather, and he wanted to get it right for the sake of Noelle's safety.

Five minutes turned into ten. The metal clip that was supposed to be used to keep the shoulder strap stable was next to impossible to thread onto the seat belt, and it had to be perfectly positioned to keep the backward-facing baby seat tight. Just as he was about to give up and let Heather have a go at it, the lock clicked.

He uncurled himself from the backseat with a sigh of relief. He thought Heather might be amused by his amateur attempt at securing the car seat but her expression was serious.

He flashed a self-effacing grin, hoping to lighten the moment. "Wow. That car seat really gave me a run for the money there, didn't it? My lack of experience is showing again. Is there anything about caring for an infant that is easy?" he joked.

She started to shake her head and then stopped, tipping her chin so her hazel eyes met his. "Love. Loving them is easy."

He felt her words like a swift uppercut to his jaw.

KO. Knockout.

Yes. Loving Noelle was easy. But it wasn't simple, because right now loving Noelle meant letting her go. And that was as complicated as it got.

"Yes, it is," he agreed through the catch in his throat. He reached for Noelle and fastened her into the car seat. Then he moved around to the front driver's side to open the door for Heather, allowing her to take her place behind the wheel before he moved around to the other side of the SUV. "I really appreciate everything you're doing for me," he added as he slid into the passenger seat.

"For Noelle, you mean," she responded without looking at him, her voice barely above a whisper.

It felt like a rebuke to Shawn's already raw heart. This day was getting tougher by the moment. But she was right. It wasn't about him.

"For Noelle," he agreed, hoping she couldn't hear any telltale grief in his tone.

The hour-long drive to San Antonio was made almost entirely in silence. Twice Shawn tried to make small talk, and twice the conversation quickly lapsed into stillness. It wasn't an easy silence between them, either. The air felt prickly. Shawn didn't know how Noelle managed to sleep so peacefully through it. Heather kept her attention on the road, but Shawn sensed there was more to it than good driving habits. She kept both white-knuckled fists clutched onto the steering wheel. The smooth skin at the corner of her jaw occasionally twitched with strain.

What bothered him most wasn't just that she was acting withdrawn in general, although there was that. This day wasn't going to be easy on anyone, Heather included. It was more the sense that she was purposefully withdrawing from *him*, and he didn't know why.

It had been her idea to accompany him, after all. She was here to help him, or rather, as she'd so succinctly pointed out, to help *Noelle*. But it appeared she didn't want to share any more of herself than was absolutely necessary. Shawn didn't even know how to begin to address the issue. Every time he spoke up, he ended up floundering to an awkward halt.

So much for being a friend to her. And his pastoral training was no help whatsoever, completely deserting him when he most needed it.

Heather seemed to relax as they entered the city. Her posture changed. Straightened and softened. She lost her stiffness and her eyes gleamed with anticipation.

Shawn, on the other hand, was a bundle of tense muscles and overactive nerves that twitched and tightened more and more with every mile they drove closer to their destination. He wanted to tell Heather to turn around and drive back to Serendipity…but he knew that wasn't an option. No matter how he felt about it personally, this thing needed to be done. It was the only way, the logical and rational conclusion to everything that had happened since the moment he'd first found Noelle in the manger.

But the knowing didn't make the doing any easier. Not for Shawn.

"You'll like Maggie," Heather remarked softly as she turned the SUV into the parking lot of the government building. "She's very down-to-earth and quite practical, but you can tell she really cares for the kids. And at the end of the day, that's what it's all about."

"I'm looking forward to meeting her." *No,*

he wasn't. Shawn rubbed his palms against his khaki slacks and then reached for the door handle.

"Shawn?" She reached for his shoulder, her touch hesitant and her voice quivering with emotion.

Swallowing back emotion, he turned and appraised her. She gave him an encouraging smile, but her gaze was filled with doubt.

"It's going to be okay," she murmured.

"Yeah." His voice dropped an octave and turned the consistency of harsh gravel. He wasn't sure he believed her. He didn't even know if *she* believed her own words.

She slid her hand down the length of his arm until her palm met his. Her hands were tiny and fragile and her fingers shook as they squeezed his. Here she was trying to make him feel better when she was probably struggling herself. This wasn't easy for either of them. Suddenly he felt as though he ought to be the one doing the reassuring. Somehow that thought infused him with courage. His hand closed over hers and she tightened her grip. Their gazes met and locked, giving and taking.

Abruptly, she broke the moment, snatching her hand from his and practically tumbling out the door in her haste to put distance between them.

"We're going to be late," she said, her voice sounding high and squeaky.

He slid a hand over his hair, feeling oddly as if something precious had been taken away from him. He didn't know what had just happened, but it had nothing to do with needing to get to the social services office. Yet what else could he do but go along with her?

"Right. I'll get the baby."

Thankfully, it was easier to remove Noelle from her car seat than it was to put her into it, and soon they were approaching Maggie Dockerty's office, such as it was. There was no receptionist at the front desk, only a clipboard with a lined sign-in sheet dangling off the front counter by a worn chain. A felt-tip pen was attached by a piece of Velcro.

Shawn glanced around. A couple of raw, informal cubicles were sectioned off by gray partitions that looked as though they'd seen better days. Hand-me-down office equipment littered the area. The whole place felt old and decrepit, not at all what Shawn would have expected from an office dedicated to finding children good homes.

A middle-aged brunette with short, spiky hair popped her head around the corner of the nearest partition. "Heather? It's good to see you again. And you must be Shawn O'Riley," she continued, nodding his direction. "Come on back and take a seat here. I'm anxious to meet that precious little baby girl Heather has been telling me all about."

Maggie's tone and words set Shawn's mind at ease. At least she appeared to genuinely care about Noelle, to acknowledge her as a person needing care.

That was something, wasn't it?

They entered Maggie's cubicle, and Shawn offered Heather a seat before taking his own, careful not to disturb Noelle, who was sound asleep in the curve of his arm. His gaze darted from place to place and finally settled on Maggie's desk, which was littered with paper. He couldn't look at Noelle or he would simply lose it, and he didn't dare meet Maggie's eyes, afraid his distress would show. He hadn't shed tears since the day they had buried David, but right now his eyes were burning like hot coals, and it took every ounce of his will to screen his emotions.

"I've already got the papers drawn up for you, Shawn," Maggie informed him, pushing a stack of papers across the desk and into his view and waving a ballpoint pen under his nose.

"Papers?" he echoed, confused. He took the pen from her, but only because she wouldn't leave off waving it at him.

Why would they need him to sign anything? He wasn't the child's guardian. Was it because he was the one who'd found her?

"Naturally, we'll have to schedule a home visit so I can make sure you've got everything baby-proofed, but it's mostly just a formality. We don't have nearly enough foster parents, and it certainly isn't every day that a man steps up for a child the way you are right now."

Steps up? What was Maggie talking about?

He shifted his confused, questioning gaze to Heather, whose hazel eyes widened in dismay. She grimaced, her hand flying up to cover her lips.

"Oh, I'm sorry, Maggie," she blurted out. "You must have misunderstood me. Shawn was gracious enough to take care of Noelle until we could get to San Antonio, but he can't keep her. Not permanently."

"I see." Maggie pinched her mouth around the edges and tiny lines formed on her upper lip. "I beg your pardon, Shawn. I was under the impression that you'd come in today to apply to become Noelle's foster father."

"I—I can't," Shawn stammered, heat rising to his face and his throat tightening, cutting off his supply of oxygen. "I would, but I—"

"Of course. I understand." Maggie cut him off before he could finish the sentence, and he was glad of it. He didn't know how he *would* have finished that sentence if Maggie hadn't taken pity on him and interrupted when she did. It wasn't so much a matter of "wouldn't." It was a matter of "couldn't." He couldn't take care of baby Noelle. He couldn't risk it. She deserved so much better than anything he was capable of offering.

"As Heather well knows, it's difficult to foster children when you're single," Maggie continued. She smiled gratefully at Heather, but Shawn noticed the stress lines that had formed on her forehead. He imagined it wasn't an easy job for her, finding homes for all the tough foster cases she dealt with every day. No wonder she looked taxed. "Heather told me you're a pastor in addition to being a rancher, Shawn. I commend you for that, and I'm sure you're far too busy with your congregation and your ranch work to care for an infant."

"No," Shawn snapped back immediately. "It's not that at all."

Both women looked at him as if he'd grown an extra eye on his forehead, and he grimaced before apologizing for his tone. He was better than this. Taking a deep breath, he focused his attention on his voice, leveling it out to something less...*frantic*.

"What I mean to say is it's not my job that

prevents me from offering my services as a foster father to Noelle. I've come to care for her, and honestly, there is nothing I'd like more than to keep her with me. It's just that—"

For a man who made his living off words, he was having difficulty forming anything remotely resembling a coherent sentence clarifying why he couldn't take Noelle. The rationalization for his choice was murky in his own mind. He only knew that he couldn't risk Noelle's safety, never mind her happiness, on his potential inabilities.

"You don't have to explain," Maggie assured him. "It's completely understandable. Believe me, I was completely aware that what I was asking you to do went far above and beyond what most folks could muster." She wheeled her office chair over to the file cabinet in the corner of her cubicle and opened the third drawer down, riffling through several multicolored folders before she selected an olive-green one. "Let me just find the papers we need to get Noelle enrolled in a state home and I'll take her off your hands."

"A state home?" Shawn repeated, his heart suddenly coming alive in his chest, beating a wild, irregular tattoo marked by rapid shots of adrenaline. The fight-or-flight instinct was kicking in, though he wasn't sure why. "I thought—

That is, I assumed she'd go to a nice foster home. With someone like Heather."

He heard a little gasp from Heather but he didn't look at her. His gaze was focused entirely on Maggie, who was frowning and shaking her head.

"As you can well imagine, there aren't enough people like Heather in the world. I'm afraid we have a serious overflow of foster children right now and not nearly enough homes for them. The procedure is that kids are temporarily assigned to state facilities until we can find potential foster families for them or they get permanently adopted, which doesn't happen nearly enough. Noelle being a newborn plays in her favor, though. Folks are more interested in adopting newborns than the older kids like Heather's taken. There's that working for her, at least. She may not have to stay in the state home for long."

"How long are we talking?" Shawn asked gravely. "A few days?"

"Weeks, more like. Sometimes months. It's hard to say. Noelle will have to be formally evaluated by one of our physicians. Often in cases of abandonment, the baby has been exposed to illegal substances in utero, which makes placement more difficult due to the medical issues drug babies face."

Shawn was stunned into silence, but his mind was screaming. Noelle in a group home with a bunch of other kids? What kind of care would she receive? How many adults would be there? Who would love her?

"A drug baby. Well, that might explain a lot," Heather murmured. "About Noelle, I mean. It could be that she's crying so often because she's in physical withdrawal from her mother's drug or alcohol habit."

"It's definitely a possibility," Maggie affirmed. "I'll make a notation in her file and we'll get her a checkup immediately so we know what we're dealing with. Now, if I can get some information from you, Shawn, I'll get this new paperwork in motion."

"No."

Maggie's green eyes snapped to his, her dark, contoured eyebrows displaying a high arch. "I beg your pardon?"

"No. I don't want Noelle going into a state facility."

Heather placed a hand on his forearm, which was a measure of comfort against the anxiety coursing through him that had him feeling as if he was about ready to jump out of his skin. Somehow she seemed to understand what was happening to him. Maybe she could see it. Every muscle in his body was crackling with energy. He was walking the proverbial plank with his hands tied out in front of him and manacles bound to his ankles.

But what else could he do?

"I'm afraid we don't have any other options," Maggie informed him crisply. "Group homes are an unfortunate by-product of the system, but I assure you that we'll do all we can to make sure Noelle is well cared for. Texas has a strong support system. Her potential problems notwithstanding, I'm optimistic that she'll eventually be placed in a permanent home. There's nothing for you to worry about."

Nothing for him to worry about?

The lady was clean out of her mind if she thought Shawn was capable of *not worrying* after handing an innocent baby off to her with no guarantee of where Noelle would land. It wasn't as if he could simply walk out of the office and forget he'd ever found the infant in the manger Christmas Eve. As if he could somehow put it all behind him and go on with his life.

"'Eventually' isn't good enough for me," Shawn informed her, adjusting Noelle in his arms so his hold on her was even more secure. Right next to his heart, where she belonged—at least for now. "I'm taking her home with me."

* * *

Heather's pulse jolted to life at Shawn's words. He was going to step up and foster baby Noelle, after all?

What man did that—set aside his own expectations, his own lifestyle, to care for the needs of another, especially one as innocent and helpless as Noelle?

None that she'd ever known. He was a rarity, for sure.

Shawn had already surprised her a number of times over the past weekend, beginning with the moment he'd volunteered to take Noelle into his care rather than pawn her off onto someone else on Christmas Eve. It would have been easy enough to hand her off to the police, or try to find someone else in town to take the baby on temporarily. But he hadn't done that. He cared enough to sacrifice his own comfort to do the right thing, even when the going got rough. And then later, after being exposed to the truth about parenthood, he hadn't broken. No matter how tired and sleep-deprived he'd been, he had never once lost his temper, yelled or complained—at least that she had heard.

And now, even after learning firsthand how difficult taking care of a newborn could be— very possibly a newborn with unforeseen medical problems—he was going to take the ultimate leap into foster parenthood.

What kind of man would make such a sacrifice?

Apparently, she was looking at him. She just couldn't believe her eyes. Or her ears. Never mind what her heart was telling her.

Shawn was a man whose actions spoke louder than his words. He was a man who saw the worth in a tiny bundle of humanity who'd been thrown out to be eaten up by the big, wide, nasty world—and he not only noticed, but stepped up to do something about it. When Noelle had been abandoned, Shawn was there to protect and defend her.

In short, he very much appeared to be the kind of man Heather had once hoped and believed existed somewhere in the world but had long since given up on finding in reality. At least, *her* reality.

The jury is still out, she reminded herself sternly. She winced inwardly. She knew better than most that what a woman observed on the outside was not always what she got on the inside, not when push came to literal shove.

"Give me a pen," Shawn said, his voice a deep, rich hum. "I'm ready to sign whatever legal documents are necessary to keep Noelle with me."

"Excellent," Maggie said. Unlike Heather, Maggie didn't sound surprised that Shawn had changed his mind—or rather, made up his mind. But then again, thinking back over Maggie's comments, Heather wondered if Maggie had been pushing Shawn that direction all along.

"Are you sure?" Heather couldn't help but ask the question aloud.

Did he realize what he was getting himself into?

He'd come with the intention of handing Noelle off to another foster family, which of course was to be expected. Why should he change his whole life because he'd found a baby inside his church? Noelle wasn't supposed to be his problem.

But now she would be. He was making her his problem, legally and officially. And Heather couldn't imagine why.

She was well aware of why *she* fostered children, or at least why she'd taken Jacob, Missy and Henry in the first place. Her motives had shifted over the months she'd had the kids, as she'd fallen in love with the three little sweethearts. But that didn't negate the fact that originally she'd signed up as a foster mother as a meager form of penitence. She wasn't kidding herself about her motivation. While she would never be able to make up for the lives lost due to her negligence with Adrian, she could and did make her foster children's lives better.

They were happy. She was as content as she'd ever been. And she loved her kids more than she'd thought possible.

But what were Shawn's motives?

God presumably knew, but Heather certainly didn't. If the pensive expression on Shawn's face was anything to go by, she doubted even Shawn knew.

Shawn patted Noelle's back in a gentle rhythm. "You mentioned baby-proofing my house." He grimaced, cleared his throat and flashed a weak grin. "How do I do that, exactly? Do you have an instruction guide? Diagrams?"

"The best I can offer you is a policy-and-procedure manual," Maggie said with a laugh. "We offer weekly parenting classes, but I'm not sure how feasible that would be for you, living as far out of town as you do."

"I'll manage," he said. The corner of his lips twitched with strain.

"I'll help," Heather assured him, even though it went against the grain to make the offer. She had enough on her plate without getting more involved in Shawn's drama, but even though she didn't feel entirely comfortable with him, who else would be there to help him prepare his living situation for Noelle, if not her? "It's really not that complicated. We'll need to cover all the open electrical outlets and put child-locks on the cabinets. You'll definitely want to move any harmful chemicals out of the reach of little hands and make sure any medicine bottles and firearms are well-protected."

"I'm not a hunter, so I don't have any weapons in the house. And I'm as healthy as a horse, so I don't have any prescription medicines around."

"Any over-the-counter painkillers? Vitamins? Antacids?" Heather probed. "They're all dangerous if ingested by an infant. Childproof caps are all well and good, but they certainly aren't fail-safe."

Light dawned in his pale blue eyes, along with a flash of panic. "Oh, yeah. Right. I didn't think. What if I... That is... I don't want to miss anything." Shawn stroked his face, drawing Heather's attention to the strong line of his clean-shaven jaw. He was taking this very seriously, she had to give him that much. It made her want to reassure him.

"You won't. I remember how overwhelmed I felt when I first brought my three kids home. Just remember you aren't alone. I'm here to help, just like I've been since Noelle came into our lives. Just a phone call away, day or night."

"You will never even begin to comprehend

how much that means to me," he replied, brushing a kiss against Noelle's dark hair.

"Oh, I think I do," Heather murmured. She couldn't help but smile at the admittedly adorable picture Shawn made, his expression as helpless as the baby in his arms.

"Is it all right if we stop at a discount store before we leave San Antonio? I'm going to need to buy a crib and a car seat immediately, and then you can help me make a list of the other supplies I'll be needing."

Heather chuckled. "Put diapers at the top of that list. Lots and lots of diapers."

The neighbors who'd visited on Christmas Day had provided enough diapers, bottles, packages of formula and changes of clothes to get Shawn and Noelle by for a while, but Heather knew there would be numerous challenges in the days ahead, and she knew she would be able to help, even if it pained her to do so.

"Diapers. Right." Shawn made a face. "Guess it goes with the territory."

"Give it a week," she advised. "Soon it'll come second nature and you won't have to think about it."

He didn't look convinced, but the glow in his eyes exhibited his resolve. He was clearly going to make a go of it on willpower alone, if nothing else.

"We can make a quick stop at Emerson's Hardware once we get back into Serendipity. They carry all the baby-proofing items we'll need. Right now Noelle is too small to get into too much mischief, but it's only a matter of time before she'll be crawling around your house. You'll need to evaluate with an eye to what a baby might get into or be harmed by. Glass furniture, sharp edges, potentially hot surfaces, even the toilet bowl. That kind of thing."

"And that will be the purpose of my visit, as well," Maggie added. "Simply to ensure Noelle's long-term well-being—not that I have any doubts, mind you. I already have a really great feeling about this particular matchup."

Shawn glanced down at Noelle and a smile played at the corners of his lips. "Blessed by the Almighty's hand."

"Perhaps," Maggie agreed mildly. "It certainly looks that way."

"I don't know why He picked me."

That statement was somewhat enlightening. Was that what this was about? Shawn having some kind of guilt complex because he'd been the one to find Noelle? Was he doing this because he thought God had somehow ordered the circumstances, practically depositing Noelle in Shawn's lap? How long would that conviction last—and what would it mean for Noelle in the aftermath?

"In any event, I assure you it's not my intention to judge you or your home in any way except to make suggestions on how to keep Noelle safe and sound. I hope you'll consider me your partner in this."

"Safe and sound," Shawn repeated with a nod. "My primary goal."

Heather's stomach turned over but she managed a light laugh despite her misgivings. "And surrounded by love. Don't forget your main concern as a foster father will be to love her."

His eyes widened on her, his shock evident. "I didn't forget," he assured her. "Loving Noelle—well, that's just a given. It's not going to slip my mind or anything. I don't have to work on that part."

"No, I don't think you do," Heather agreed, and she was astounded to find she actually believed him. This guy was quite literally putting his life on hold for this child. Perhaps there was good in the world after all.

Chapter Five

Shawn jammed a pitchfork into a bale of hay and tossed it into the nearest stall, then repeated the process for the three stalls down the line. His Shetland sheepdog, the Queen of Sheba—Queenie, for short—followed at his heels, barking. It was a little more complicated to pitch hay and carry feed with an infant strapped to his chest, but he hadn't figured out what else he could do with Noelle while he worked, and the animals had to be fed.

Morning and evening, he and Noelle were out in the barn doing chores.

In addition to his three horses, he owned a brood of chickens, seven stubborn, lawn-mower-worthy goats, six sows—and at the moment, a dozen piglets. It didn't pay to own a boar, so he just borrowed one from the neighbors when the time was ripe.

He loved his work as a pastor, but ranching was in his blood. And while he didn't have time to care for a herd of cattle, his pigs and goats brought in a tidy hobby income and he had plenty of opportunities to ride and rope and mend fences helping friends, neighbors and congregants with their stock. Still, on a regular daily basis it was fairly lonely work. He actually liked having human company, even that of a little human. Over the week since he'd officially become a foster father, he'd learned to adapt all the components of his busy lifestyle to the baby's needs.

It was a mild day, and he'd bundled Noelle in long-sleeved terry-cloth pink pajamas, complete with footies. His kid was cute. Adorable. His breath crammed into his throat every time he looked at the little darlin'.

He had just finished slopping the pigs when Heather's silver SUV turned into his long driveway. He waved to her and she returned the gesture with a jerky nod.

Shawn's breath caught. There it was again. That gut *feeling* he had—as if something was amiss between the two of them, only it was all on Heather's side and he didn't know why. Had he done something?

"We have company, baby darlin'," he informed Noelle, who noisily sucked her fist in response. He grinned and tossed the feed bucket into the barn, hurrying to help Heather get the kids out of the car.

"I'm glad you brought the kiddos along with you," he said as she rounded them to her side. "I think they'll like the ranch."

"It was your idea, remember?" she reminded him with a dry chuckle.

"I know, right?" he agreed, joining his laughter to hers. "I figured it would be easier for you to bring them along than try to find alternate care for them."

"Easier for me, perhaps," she agreed, "but I'm not going to guarantee it will be easier for you. These kids are a handful and a half." She didn't sound as if it bothered her—only that she believed it might bother him.

Shawn didn't think it would be a problem. He liked kids, and they usually seemed to take to him. He'd gotten along with Heather's kids on Christmas Day just fine. He knelt to the children's level. "I have a surprise for you. Do you want to see what it is?"

Missy immediately nodded and slipped her tiny hand into his, her smile eager and trusting. Little Henry looked from him to Heather and back again, seeking direction on whether or not it was okay to go with this man. He stared at Shawn with wide brown eyes, his thumb in his mouth, and then opted to crawl into Heather's arms instead of taking Shawn's other hand.

Jacob's demeanor was also less than enthusiastic. He frowned and slinked back at Shawn's words, shifting his attention from Shawn to the barn to his shoes, but not before Shawn thought he glimpsed the hint of interest in the boy's eyes. Shawn prayed silently for the poor kid. He imagined Jacob had been through a lot in his young life. It was no wonder he was hesitant.

He knew firsthand what it was to be a young man with no one to depend on but himself. After they'd lost David, Shawn's mother hadn't been there at all, and his dad had been mostly out of the picture with his drinking habit. At least Jacob had Heather now. She provided the love and stability Shawn had never had as a child. For whatever reason, Heather had dedicated herself to these three foster kids, and they were blessed to have her. He hoped they'd someday realize what they had.

"Come with me and we'll grab a baby bottle out of the barn," he said, regaining his feet and pointing toward the large red structure.

"You keep your baby formula in the barn?" Heather asked, her voice an even mixture of astonishment and horror.

Shawn laughed and shook his head. "Not

exactly. Although, come to think of it, I imagine Noelle will be ready to eat pretty soon here, too."

"Too?"

Shawn raised his eyebrows and flashed Heather what he hoped was a mysterious grin. "It's easier for you to see what I'm talking about than for me to try to explain. Why don't you all follow me and I'll show you what I mean."

He led the way into the shadow of the barn, scooping up the bottle he'd prepared off a shelf just inside the door, and then glanced over his shoulder to make sure Heather followed. She was just behind him, holding three-year-old Henry on one hip and tugging a reluctant Jacob along with her opposite arm.

"Have you spent any time on a ranch? Do you like farm animals?" Shawn asked, directing his question at nine-year-old Jacob.

The boy shrugged noncommittally and didn't quite meet his gaze.

"Horses?" Shawn prodded. "Goats? Chickens? Pigs?"

"Piggies!" seven-year-old Missy exclaimed, tugging on her blond ponytail and twirling on her toes like a tiny ballerina.

"Piggies it is, then," Shawn agreed, his grin widening. At least the little girl seemed excited about her day. He'd have to work on the other two.

Heather wrinkled her nose. "I was raised on a ranch here in Serendipity, but I can't say taking care of the animals was one of my favorite chores."

"No?" Her statement caught Shawn off guard, and he shuffled to a stop, tossing a look over his right shoulder to see if she was teasing him. Her lips were pinched together in a straight line that accentuated the crease in her eyebrows. She was far too young to have the kind of worry lines she displayed.

He had to admit his surprise. He would have pegged her for an animal lover. She had that sensitive nature about her. She was a small woman with a delicate physique, so it wasn't as if he expected she would go all-in for heavy ranch labor, but for some reason he'd supposed she would enjoy spending time around the animals. In fact, he'd banked this whole day on that assumption. "So you're not a fan of farm animals, then?"

"No, not really. Is that a terrible thing to say? I was incredibly jealous of my older sister, Havanah. All she had to do was wash dishes every evening, while I was responsible for getting up at the crack of dawn every single day to milk the dairy cow. Rain or shine, hot or cold, in school or on summer vacation, three hundred sixty-five days a year." She scrunched her lips in distaste.

Shawn chuckled. "That bad, huh?"

"Considering I am not, never have been and never will be a morning person? Yes. Definitely *that bad*. It wasn't the milking I minded so much, or the cow, for that matter. Hershey, our milk cow, was my confidant. Free therapy to go along with the benefits of calcium."

"And chocolate milk?" he teased.

She chuckled. "I wish. It's been a long time since I thought about my life back then. Those were definitely the good old days."

He laughed. "You are far too young to have 'good old days.'"

"Well, thank you, but you're wrong about that."

Her eyes met Shawn's, and for the briefest beat he had a glimpse of her vulnerability—and her pain. She did look older than her age, but only in the depths of her gaze. He suspected she'd seen too much, lived too hard.

She shook her head and scoffed, and the moment passed.

"Listen to me going on as if my high school years were something special. I had as much teenage angst as anyone—as Hershey well knew." Her laugh was forced and unnatural, but the sigh that followed after was real enough.

"I couldn't stand the daybreak part of the equation. Some mornings I wanted to pelt something at those roosters when they started their annoying crowing. Ugh. Country living definitely has its pitfalls."

He'd never thought of it that way. He liked the roosters and God's brilliant sunrises. He saw happiness in the start of a new day, where she observed the drawbacks.

Everything positive in his life that made it the joy it was centered around country living. The seven years he'd spent in the city going to college and seminary were the longest of his life. He'd enjoyed school, but he missed the clean air, the hard work—and the animals.

Where ranching was concerned, he supposed it didn't hurt that he was a morning person. He'd never thought twice about rising before dawn to care for the stock. He would be up even if he didn't have to be. It was easy for him. Enjoyable.

But not so much for Heather. He got that, and he felt bad that he'd already evidently brought back unpleasant memories for her. He didn't want to make it worse. But what were they really talking about? He could feel in his gut that there was much she was not telling him, and whatever the subtext was, it had little to do with small-town living or even getting up in the morning. He wished he could read between the lines, understand what she was *not* telling him.

The fact that she'd come back to live in Serendipity after moving away for whatever reason was telling in itself. She obviously didn't dislike sprawling ranch land enough to stay away—although the fact that she lived in town and didn't own a cow that needed daily milking might have been a factor, as well. Yet now she was caring for children. As he had learned with Noelle, children ran on their own timetables. What made that more palatable to her than the timetable of ranch life?

He wondered if he'd made a tactical error inviting her into his barn. Baby-proofing the house was one thing. Stomping around with the animals was quite another.

Maybe she'd think his operation was lame, or worse, it would remind her of not-so-happy days. He hesitated, rethinking his options, but in the end, he plunged into the shadow of the barn, passed the three horses and then turned left into a stall that was...*otherwise* occupied.

No horses here.

The children would like his surprise, he was certain of it. And whether or not it was precisely what she would have chosen, he suspected Heather would be pleased with the outcome, simply because he expected it would include seeing her kids all bubbly and full of joy.

Inside the stall, lounging on a fresh bed of hay, were a plump mama sow and twelve little black-and-white-spotted piglets. Just a few days old, they were only just beginning to sprout hair. Most of them were grunting and rooting for their mother's milk, but one little piglet, the tiniest of the bunch, was consistently squeezed out, no matter how often he attempted to dive into the middle of the fray.

"See this little fellow here?" Shawn asked, dropping to his knees before the pigs and scooping the runt into his hand. "His big brothers and sisters aren't letting him have a turn for a meal. How fair is that? We're going to help him out a little bit so he can grow big and strong like his siblings."

Missy cheered, clearly delighted with the idea. Both boys leaned in to see what Shawn was going to do next. He was happy all the kids were interested, but his eyes were on Heather's reaction.

"You're feeding the runt of the litter?" She squatted down beside him. Even though the hay was clean and freshly tossed, she didn't actually kneel in it. He noticed how carefully she chose her footing, despite the fact that she was wearing cowboy boots that looked as though they'd seen their fair share of use. She'd spent the past several years in the city—a country girl who'd possibly been displaced a little too long? Was that why she was so uncomfortable with her surroundings?

Shawn forced a grin and winked at her, hoping to ease the tension between them. "I figure everyone ought to try to help the weak ones among us."

Heather gave a surprised gasp and her hazel eyes widened on him. It was the oddest look, and it made him uncomfortable.

"That's so…wonderful," she murmured.

Shawn lifted a brow. It was just a pig, after all.

Or were they no longer speaking of barnyard animals? She was staring at him as if he'd just said he was single-handedly conquering world hunger. He couldn't mistake the admiration shining from her gaze, and for some reason it simultaneously choked him up and revved up his ego, which was going to swell to the size of Texas if he didn't avert his eyes from the smile softly forming on the curve of her mouth. Her lips didn't need gloss or color to shine—just happy thoughts.

"Do you want to do the honors?" he asked Missy, pressing the bottle into the little girl's hands. Anything to get his mind away from the myriad distractions of Heather's outstanding facial features.

Eyes. Lips. Straight, narrow nose. Good grief. He was getting carried away.

The seven-year-old gripped the bottle tightly, her small, pink tongue pressing out from between her lips as she concentrated on aiming the working end of the container at the piglet's snout. What a cute little darlin' she was.

The girl. Not the pig. Well, the pig was kind of cute, too. And the other children, including his precious Noelle.

Okay, the woman was pretty decent, as well.

Aaand there he went again.

"I named him Hammie," he told Missy as the piglet rooted for the nipple.

Heather snorted. "Hammie? Really?"

Heat crept up Shawn's neck. "All right. I'll admit that's not the most original name I could have come up with."

"Of course it is. H-Hammie. For—" The end of her sentence was cut off by another sputter of laughter. She pressed her thumb and forefinger to her eyes. "And I suppose you've also got Bacon and Pork Chop somewhere in this bunch."

She snorted. *Snorted*. And Shawn didn't think he'd ever heard anything so adorable.

"Honestly, I think it's cute that you named him."

Cute?

Well, at least he had her laughing, and it was the real thing, for once. Their eyes met and held. She grinned at him, a genuine smile that made his gut spring into a series of gymnastic flips he found difficult to tame. What was it about this woman? He'd never felt so off-kilter in his life.

"I've named all my animals," he admitted, wondering just how silly he must look to her. His ego shriveled. "I know that sounds kind of dumb, but it helps me keep them straight in my mind. Otherwise the goats just blend into a mass of spots and I don't know who's been fed and who's still hungry. Although with the goats, they are always hungry." He chuckled at his own joke.

"I would imagine so," she said, smothering a laugh with her palm. "I seem to recall our goats eating anything and everything. Grass. Clothing. Shoes."

"Right? The goats keep my grass nice and trimmed, but I've got to watch them or they get into mischief."

"Me feed Hammie?" Henry asked, lisping the words around the thumb he hadn't bothered to remove from his mouth before he spoke. "Me do it. Me want to feed the piggy." He'd gone from a simple "May I" question to downright insistence in less than one second.

"Sure you can, big guy," he said, trying to counter the sudden turning of Henry's emotions. The boy looked as if he was about one step short of a tantrum. Shawn wasn't quite sure what to do with a three-year-old, and he shifted his gaze to Heather for help.

"It's 'May I,'" Heather corrected, her voice equal parts firm and soothing. "Missy, will you please allow Henry to have a turn?"

Shawn prepared himself for Missy to have an equally volatile temper. Seeing the gentle way she cradled the piglet in her arms, he expected her to have some trouble sharing this experience, but the little girl immediately nodded.

"Guess so," she said, sounding only a little bit disappointed.

"I'll tell you what, Missy," Shawn said, not liking the way his own heart dipped upon hearing the little girl's reluctance to give up the task, "you and your foster brothers can come over to visit the piggies whenever your mama says it's okay."

He helped the two children facilitate the transfer of the piglet and bottle between hands. Heather shifted sideways to come between Missy and Henry, ready to lend a hand if necessary. A whiff of roses reached Shawn's nostrils, a startling contrast to the sharp tang of barn smells. He struggled not to lean in toward Heather and discover whether the scent was coming from her shampoo or her perfume. Either way, it knocked his socks off. Way better than the smell of horses.

"Jacob?" He didn't want to press the boy, but he also didn't want him to feel left out. "If you'd like a turn then you're up next, after Henry."

Jacob grunted and shook his dark head. "That's okay. I don't want to." He scowled, and for a moment Shawn thought he was about to let loose on all cannons. Then he shrugged and turned away from the adults. "No, really. Let Missy and Henry feed it. No big deal."

Jacob sounded as if he wasn't having any fun at all, and Shawn's heart gave a little tug for the boy, who not only carried wisdom beyond his years in his gaze but also had to step up to the plate for his younger "siblings," displaying a maturity quite remarkable for his age.

"I can see what a good foster brother you are, looking out for Missy and Henry all the time," Shawn said, laying a hand on Jacob's shoulder. "Your mama must be very proud of you."

Jacob shrugged his hand away, trying to look as if it didn't matter to him one way or the other what anyone thought, but when he shook his dark hair back, Shawn could see his blue eyes were alight with pleasure from the commendation.

"I depend on Jacob for the big jobs," Heather assured him.

The boy stubbed his toe into the ground, his hair falling across his forehead.

"He's the regular man of the house. I couldn't do without him."

Shawn didn't have to be particularly observant to see how much Heather's praise meant to Jacob. Pride was flashing there in his eyes for everyone to see. His shoulders straightened and he stood up a good inch taller, his gaze full of strength and determination. He was the *man of the house*.

Shawn grinned, but he was sad for Heather. Jacob was a good boy, but he was nine. He couldn't be protector and provider for her or his younger foster siblings, and he shouldn't have to be. Shawn understood more than most the weight of responsibility that came with caring for a sibling. He wondered how Heather carried such a burden, and if she sought God for help. Even if her relationship with the Lord was rock-solid, being a single foster mother to three children would be tough for any woman.

"Got to watch over the little ones," Jacob stated with a resolute nod. "Otherwise they won't have anyone."

Heather absently brushed Jacob's black hair off his forehead with her fingertips. "See? That's exactly what I'm saying. You're a good boy, and you know better than anybody that you kids need to stick together. I'm so proud of you, Jacob. You children mean everything to me." She sniffed, and Shawn thought she might have brushed a tear aside with a casual flick of her hand.

Jacob colored and made a big production out of stooping down to pet Queenie, who barked with a high-pitched yap that startled Noelle. Shawn gently bounced her with the palm of his hand, coaxing her back to sleep. Queenie nipped at the boy's heels with the natural instinct of a herding breed. Shawn noted the glassy appearance of Jacob's eyes, and he hid his smile. Heather was clearly not the only one sniffling over the emotional discourse. Even Shawn's throat felt a little rough with emotion.

Time to take the conversation in a new direction. The last thing Shawn wanted was for Heather to burst into tears. Even in his pastoral duties, he never had been good at handling a crying woman. And she wasn't the only one he was worried about.

He well remembered what it was like to be nine years old and having to man-up against his father's perpetual drunkenness and his mother's absence from his life. He knew the last thing a young boy like Jacob would want would be to be caught with tears in his eyes, especially since Heather had just singled him out as being the man of the house. At least with Jacob that title was an honor and not a curse.

"You know, it sounds like I'm the exact opposite of you." Shawn pulled Heather's attention toward him so Jacob would get the heat taken off him and have a moment to pull himself together.

Henry's attention had already wavered, and the piglet rolled out of his lap and onto the hay. Missy had wandered off to follow Jacob and Queenie, leaving poor Hammie to squeal and squirm.

"Really? How's that?" Heather asked, taking pity on the piglet. She scooped it up and cradled it in her arms, much as she did when she was holding Noelle. The woman had nurturer written all over her, from her body language to her expression to the soft, sweet gaze in her eyes.

"This baby pig is outright adorable," she commented. "Look at him. He's wagging his little tail just like a happy puppy."

He'd mistakenly thought she wouldn't want a turn holding Hammie, seeing as she was so skittish around the barn. She wouldn't even put her knees into the hay—and yet she was willing to cradle a pig?

Shawn didn't understand women, and he was especially thick where Heather was concerned, but he was happy to relieve Henry of the bottle and pass it to her, especially since Henry was now completely distracted and caught up playing with Queenie, just as the other children were.

"We were discussing ranch chores before," he explained. "You mentioned you never much liked the early-morning rooster calls and the need to get up and milk the cow, whereas I've always found great solace in taking care of the animals. Granted, I didn't enjoy mucking stalls any better than any other boy or girl of my acquaintance," he said, gently adjusting the angle of the bottle in Heather's hand so Hammie had better access to it. Babies and pigs were slightly different in that respect. "But I didn't mind getting up in the early hours. I still rise before the sun—and probably would even if I didn't have stock to attend to."

It was true that he hadn't ever talked to his animals the way Heather apparently had as a teen—not out loud, at any rate—but he suspected more than one of the cows and horses from his childhood had known the secret pain of his teenage heart. Hadn't he spent many hours in the saddle as a child trying to escape the reality of his life? "I've always found it rather peaceful, out there all alone in the barn, just me and the animals. You know?"

He paused, shook his head and laughed at himself. "What am I saying? Of course you know—from personal experience. Like I said, we're opposites."

"We may not be as different as you think. Granted, there are things I'd rather be doing at that time of day," she acknowledged. "Like catching some extra z's, for example." Her lips tipped up at the corners, but amusement didn't quite reach her gaze. "It wasn't that I hated it, exactly. I'll admit there's something to be said about having had regular chores growing up. Ranch work taught me responsibility at an early age, which is never a bad thing. And I learned that sometimes it was necessary to perform my duties even on those days when I wasn't real keen on it. Those lessons have served me in good stead now that I have to work for a living. You can't exactly call your boss and tell him you don't want to go to work today because it's too early and you don't feel like it, right? I work at home as a virtual assistant, so some days I have even more of a challenge motivating myself to get the job done. And that's before getting into what's involved in being Mama to these busy, energetic children. They don't ever take a day off. I definitely can't decide to walk away from my obligations with them, nor would I want to."

Her gaze shifted back to Jacob and the corners of her lips dropped into a frown. "Perhaps I should have given the idea of buying a ranch more than a passing thought when I moved back to Serendipity. It occurred to me, but I didn't spend too much time thinking about it. My little house is relatively easy to keep clean, or at least as neat as a home with three children can be, but it would have been nice to have something more physical to offer my kids, especially Jacob. I think he could use something challenging to dig into. He's got so much energy, and I'd like for him to have something positive and constructive to do with his free time."

A thought occurred to him, but he wanted to be able to discuss it with Heather before sharing it in front of the children. He wanted to offer her the opportunity to bring the kids over on a regular basis to interact with the animals and learn ranching skills—if the idea appealed to Heather.

"Kids, I've also got kittens. Two doors that direction," he said, pointing to a corner on the other side of the barn. "Little gray tabbies. Only a couple of weeks old. You ought to go take a look."

"Look, but don't touch," Heather amended. Shawn appreciated how she was always on top of the parenting thing. He wasn't certain he had that same ability. Observing Heather at work was better than a college course in parenting skills.

Jacob took Henry's and Missy's hands and led the way across the barn to where Shawn had indicated. He smiled when he heard their mutual exclamations of delight. Even Jacob sounded excited at the furry find.

Heather smiled, as well. Still in a crouch, she shifted her weight so Hammie was more safely entrenched in her arms, then lost her balance and fell forward onto her knees in the hay. A lock of her glossy brown hair escaped from the low clasp of her ponytail and fell over her forehead. Her arms were full trying to restrain the wiggling piglet, so she tweaked her chin and blew at the stubborn strand in an unsuccessful attempt to get it out of her eyes.

Without pausing to give it any real thought, Shawn reached forward to brush her hair behind her ear for her. His fingertips barely grazed her temple, but she tossed the bottle and jerked backward as if he'd physically slapped her, her heels raising dust and hay from the ground. She lost her air in an audible huff when her bottom hit the solid floor of the stable. Hammie squealed and squirmed out of her grasp.

"I'm so sorry. I—" Shawn stammered. Heat rose to his cheeks as he scrambled to his feet and reached for the woman sprawled across the hay in an undignified heap with one hand, cradling Noelle with the other. His arms and his expression pleaded with Heather. "I didn't— I wasn't trying to—"

Heather shook her head violently and scuttled backward until her back met the stable door. She inhaled again, another audibly terrified sweep of air. Her hazel eyes were wide and glassy. She was staring straight at him, but it was almost as if she were looking through him. Shawn had the distinct impression it wasn't his face she was seeing.

His breath felt glued to the inside of his lungs and anxiety banded around his chest.

Lord, help me. What had he done?

She reminded him of a frightened doe cornered by a mountain lion. That he was the mountain lion in this scenario made him sick to his stomach. She was frozen in place and yet visibly quivering, ruffling Shawn to the core of his being.

He became intensely aware of his every movement, afraid he was going to make things worse. Slowly, carefully, he lifted his hands in a gesture of surrender so she would recognize he was no threat to her. He waited silently as she visibly took control of her thoughts and her breathing. Gradually, the bright beacons of alarm faded from her gaze. Slowly, she released her clenched fists and uncoiled herself from her defensive position, wobbling slightly as she regained her feet. She snatched Hammie from the floor and held him close to her heart, whispering comforting nonsense syllables to the tiny, wiggling piglet. Shawn suspected the reassurance was more for her than it was for the pig.

He searched his mind for the right thing to say but came up blank. He sensed that they were at a defining moment in their dubious friendship.

If he said the wrong thing now, she'd be out of his life so fast his head would spin. And then where would he be? As selfish as it sounded, he was absolutely positive he wouldn't be able to be a good foster father to Noelle without Heather's assistance.

But never mind how it might affect him. His primary concern right now was how *Heather* was feeling. What had happened in her past to make her have that marked and painful of a reaction to his touch?

And how could he help?

Whatever it was, it must have been horrible.

It had to have been a man who had hurt her at some point. Fury rose in Shawn's chest. He wanted to grab whoever had done this to her by the collar and shake him senseless. Tension rippled through his body, and he had to force himself to relax and not clench his fists.

Deeply aware of how any violence in his actions would look to her, he jammed his hands into the back pockets of his jeans and rocked back on his heels, waiting for her to make the first move. He was glad the children were two stable doors down so they weren't witnessing their foster mother's distress. He was certain they would have picked up on the fact that she was shaken to the core. Kids were sensitive that way.

"I, um—" Her voice wobbled. She ran a hand down her face, then pinched the bridge of her nose and sighed. "I imagine you're probably wondering why I completely freaked out on you just now."

"I wouldn't put it quite that way," he corrected gently.

"No? What would you call it, then? I just made a complete and total spectacle of myself in front of you. I've never been so humiliated in my life."

"Heather." How could he comfort her without touching her? "I don't want you to worry about me. You have absolutely no reason to feel embarrassed. None whatsoever. I'm not judging you at all—I promise. I care. I really do."

Her gaze snapped to his. He stood absolutely stock-still as she cautiously took his measure. After an extended pause, she nodded and then reached a tentative hand toward his forearm. Her fingers quivered and she tightened her grip. "You're right. I know this about you. I do."

"You know...*what* about me?" he asked, not certain he was following her train of thought. In fact, he knew he wasn't keeping up to the recoil of her emotions. She'd gone from scrambling away from him to resolutely touching him. "I don't, um— That is—"

Stammering was not helping this situation, but he felt as if his tongue was in knots. Deep down, he experienced an agonizing physical yearning to wrap his arms around her and protect her from whatever it was that had her so rattled. It took every bit of his strength of will not to do so, and only because he knew that would be the absolute worst possible move he could make right now.

His mere touch had her both physically and emotionally somersaulting away from him. If he tried to hold her in his arms—well, that would only make things worse. He wasn't going to do that to her. He wouldn't do that to anyone, but

Heather wasn't just anyone. He couldn't explain it any more than he could explain where his faith in God came from, but he felt differently about Heather than any of the other women of his acquaintance, present or past. She was special, somehow, and he was attracted to her. But she was a package deal, three kids included.

Which was all the more reason for him to be mindful of his actions. He needed to tread extra carefully where Heather was concerned. He was hardly adequate as a foster father to Noelle. He'd never measure up to the challenge of three more needy children. They deserved an experienced hand to guide them, and he was not it.

Her eyes dropped to the piglet in her arms. "You don't understand why I'm acting so skittish," she finished for him.

He shrugged and bent his head until he could capture her gaze once again. "I'm a good listener."

"Right. Because you're a pastor."

"No. That's not why. Or at least, that's not all of it." How could he explain that his reaction to her distress had less to do with him being a pastor and a great deal more with him being a man? If he tried to convey that his feelings at the moment went beyond Christian charity, he was fairly certain he would send her running for the hills as fast as her legs could carry her. Yet he knew conversations about faith made her uncomfortable. If she felt that he was only there for her as a spiritual leader, he knew instinctively that she would clam up rather than explain her problems and fears to him.

He didn't know how much she would actually share with him, if anything, but the barn was hardly the place for a serious conversation. Much better that he invite her back up to the house, where she could sip a cup of coffee and compose herself.

"Kids?" he called, loud enough to be heard across the stable. "Anyone up for some ice cream?"

The last thing Heather wanted to do was follow Shawn back to his house. Shame filled her at the way she'd treated him, at the reactions she couldn't seem to be able to control even after all this time. He hadn't deserved her going off on him the way she had.

He'd graciously accepted her fumbling apology, but he'd closed up on her. And it was no wonder.

If it weren't for the fact that Shawn had offered the kids ice-cream sandwiches—their favorite special-occasion dessert—she would have come up with some lame excuse for why she had to leave immediately. Never mind that she wouldn't be fulfilling her obligation to do what she came here to do—namely, checking Shawn's progress on baby-proofing his house before the social worker made her official visit.

Let it go. Let it go.

Heather's heart continued to reel from the memory of Shawn's gentle touch and her own outlandish reaction. Her thoughts and emotions made her equal parts alarmed and angry. Angry that Adrian had ruined even the possibility of her responding well to a kind touch, or ever knowing love in her life, and the fear that—

Well, there it was. She'd been around Shawn enough to believe that the man he presented to the world was exactly the man he continued to be behind closed doors. With Shawn, what a woman saw was what she got. Like seeing the way he cherished Noelle, pretty much acting as if the sun and moon rose in her tiny face. He was the kind of man any normal woman would be thrilled to have a relationship with.

But she wasn't *normal*, now, was she?

Adrian had never in his life dealt with another human being the way Shawn treated virtually everyone with whom he crossed paths. Lost in the throes of his addiction, Adrian only had room in his life for one person—himself. And his scotch. The few times she'd tried to interrupt the relationship between the man and his booze had resulted in a broken wrist. Broken ribs.

Dead children.

Was it any wonder she still reacted negatively to even the slightest touch from a man? No one could blame her if she did.

But she hated it. Really, really *hated* her inability to live a normal life. She'd give anything not to have to explain to Shawn why she'd responded the way she had.

Not to live in perpetual fear.

"Food first, and then a tour of the house," Shawn said, breaking into her thoughts. Nothing about awkward explanations. He unstrapped Noelle from his chest and kissed her downy forehead. "Ice cream for the older kids, and it's a bottle of formula for you, Little Miss Noelle." He gestured to Heather and pointed to the freezer. "I've got two flavors—of ice cream, that is. Strawberry and vanilla. The children can choose whichever they like. You, too, Heather. And there's coffee in the pot by the sink. Now if you'll excuse me a moment, I have to take care of somebody's wet diaper."

Once Shawn was out of her line of vision, Heather busied herself serving ice-cream sandwiches to the children. Her stomach was too raw to take one for herself, but a warm cup of coffee sounded good. She located the pot and then went in search of mugs.

She wasn't snooping, but it was quickly evident that Shawn's cabinets were as bleak as his decor—which was to say, he had nothing. Or almost nothing.

Four mismatched glass dinner plates in one cupboard. A couple of large, fluorescent-green plastic cups graced another. She finally found two unadorned white coffee mugs in the cabinet over the sink.

"I take it you don't have many guests around here," she said to Shawn when he returned. She poured two cups from the carafe. "I could only find these two mugs for the coffee. I hope they're okay."

"They're fine. As you observed, they are our only choice."

"I thought pastors did a lot of that. Entertaining, I mean."

He plunked Noelle into the bassinet and then rummaged through the walk-in pantry, reappearing with a baby bottle in hand. Then he opened the refrigerator and removed what Heather assumed was a jug of baby formula.

"I can offer you sugar for your coffee. Sorry, no milk—unless you want a drop of this." He hefted the container of formula and chuckled.

"I'm not guaranteeing how it would taste in coffee."

"Eww." She wrinkled her nose. His teasing put her at ease. "No, that's okay. I think I'll pass."

"It's exactly like you said. I don't get visitors. I don't drink milk, so I don't buy the stuff. I suppose that'll change if I have Noelle for more than a few months." A flash of melancholy crossed his gaze, but only for a moment. Then his expression cleared and filled with so much joy Heather wondered if she'd imagined the sadness in his eyes.

"I'm sure you'll adapt," she assured him, taking a seat in the nearest kitchen chair and leaning her forearms against the table, which was littered with an assortment of baby-proofing hardware. "Look at you. You already are."

Shawn's red-gold eyebrows danced. He zapped the contents of the bottle for a few seconds, removed it from the microwave and tested the temperature of the formula against the inside of his wrist.

"See? You're a pro."

"I'm getting there. Even diaper duty isn't too bad anymore." He settled into the chair opposite her, cradling Noelle in one arm. She couldn't believe how much more comfortable he appeared with Noelle compared to the first few days he'd had with the baby.

Noelle was likewise a great deal more complacent, taking her bottle from Shawn without even a whimper of protest.

It didn't take long for Heather's kids to finish their ice cream, nor for Noelle to drain her bottle. Heather and Shawn kept up insignificant chatter, but to her, at least, there was a gigantic elephant in the room, one she knew she'd eventually have to address.

The questions were there in his eyes, even if he didn't voice them aloud.

Why had she bolted like a branded calf when he touched her?

Like the gentleman he was, he didn't press her for answers. He was clearly letting her set the pace.

"Why don't you kids go out onto the back porch and throw a stick for Queenie?" Shawn suggested as he tucked a now-sleeping Noelle into the bassinet.

"Stay where I can see you," Heather added. The sliding glass door wouldn't make it difficult to monitor the kids from where she sat in the comfort of the kitchen.

Her heart softened as she watched Shawn fuss over the baby. It was incredibly cute how he took extra care to make sure she was tightly swaddled and resting comfortably, and the nonsense syllables he babbled at her were beyond adorable. Heather suspected Noelle might nap better in the crib in her bedroom—the Jenny Lind crib she'd helped Shawn pick out the day they were in San Antonio. But from all appearances, Shawn didn't want to let Noelle out of his sight, not even for a minute.

So sweet. So loving. The man had father written all over him.

Her own father had died when she was just ten, but to her as a child, he had been a shining example of all that a man could be. She remembered him leaning in close to her mother and tickling her ribs just to see her giggle. Her father's laugh had been hearty and frequent. She idealized him, and consciously or unconsciously had been looking all her life for those qualities her father had possessed in abundance—qualities Adrian had initially seemed to share. She'd realized only too late that it was all an illusion.

A man like Shawn—handsome, clean-cut, responsible, a man of faith and a pastor—why, he ticked off every item on any woman's hypothetical Qualities to Look for in a Man list. So why hadn't some nice Christian woman come along and taken him off the market?

She didn't like how uncomfortable the thought of another woman in his life made her feel. She lifted her chin and shifted her gaze

away from him. Better that she keep her eyes
and her mind on her children, who were having a raucously good time throwing sticks for
Queenie. The dog was plenty energetic enough
to keep up with all three of them.

Silence reigned in the room, hot and thick
and heavy. This was beyond awkward. Shawn
had just seen her at her worst out there in the
barn, panicking at his mere touch even though
he'd done nothing to deserve her distrust. She
could feel his gaze upon her but didn't have the
heart to turn back to see what he was thinking.

Coward.

No, she was not a coward—not anymore.

Elephant in the room? She was going to tame
that beast right now, before the circus began.

She cleared her throat and turned her attention to him. He was, indeed, staring at her, but
it didn't unnerve her the way she expected it
to. He kept his full attention on her face. That
was something else she'd noticed about Shawn.
He looked people straight in the eye. Not so
much challenging her, but stepping up beside
her and comforting her without words or a physical touch.

She swallowed hard to remove the lump of
emotion choking the breath from her lungs and
forced the words from her mouth. "I'm sure

you're wondering why I did the—er—Texas Two-Step out in the barn earlier."

He didn't even pretend not to understand. He acknowledged her statement with a brief nod, and compassion flooded his gaze. His tenderness nearly undid her. She could not— would not—come unhinged while talking about Adrian. Her past was just that—her past. There was no way around the pain and discomfort except to plunge forward, right through the middle of it, and no amount of time or therapy would ever quite take away the sting.

"I wondered," Shawn murmured. "But I don't want to push you. If you're not ready to talk about it, that's okay. I'm here for you if you need me, but I don't want you to feel I'm pressuring you."

"Is that your pastoral training talking?" She didn't know why she said it that way. The question sounded dismissive and off-putting even to her ears. She couldn't imagine how it sounded to him.

His eyebrows shot up in surprise. "No. I don't think there is training for situations like this one. I want to be your friend, Heather, not your pastor. If you'll let me."

Could she let him?

Her heart said yes, but she didn't trust her emotions anymore.

"You probably know I was married before," she began, stumbling over her words.

He nodded but didn't interrupt.

"Well, what you don't know—it's something I don't usually talk about." She paused and squeezed her eyes shut, praying she could get through this and say the words aloud. "My ex-husband is serving time in prison."

"Is he?"

"Yes. It's where he belongs. Adrian is not a nice man, but he puts on a surprisingly effective facade. I'm embarrassed to admit I fell for it. I thought I was marrying a charming, faithful man. It was only after we'd exchanged vows that I discovered I was married to a monster."

"He was physically abusive," Shawn concluded. It hadn't taken much for him to fill in the blanks. "Which explains a lot."

"That was the least of it." Heather couldn't keep the disgust from her voice, nor the fear and pain.

"Don't say that." Shawn started to reach across the table, then abruptly stopped himself and leaned back in his chair, crossing his arms.

His gaze said it all. He believed in her. How little he knew.

"It kills me that he hurt you," Shawn said through gritted teeth. He clenched his hands into fists, and his biceps pulsed, but oddly enough, she didn't feel threatened by his posture. She felt safe. "What makes this infinitely worse is that I can see the lasting effects his abuse has had on you, showing me that he's *still* hurting you even though he's not around anymore. Honey, you're worth more than you know. To God. To your kids. To me."

Her breath scratched against her throat. She so wanted to believe his words, but he'd spoken in haste, before he'd heard the whole story. Once he had, she had no doubt his opinion of her would take a nosedive. She was too far beyond God's grace for easy redemption.

She paused. Maybe she should stop right here and not say any more. She'd said enough to explain her peculiar reaction to him in the barn. She could leave off and he'd never have to know the woman she really was.

But she wanted—well, she didn't even know what she wanted. Or at least, she couldn't put it into words. But she was certain playing the pity card wasn't going to get it for her.

Shawn had extended a genuine hand of friendship. She couldn't accept it under false pretenses, no matter how much a part of her wanted to sweep her past under the rug. No, her memories were something she would have to live with for the rest of her life.

"I need to tell you why Adrian is behind bars."

Shawn's lips quirked and his gaze flashed with anger. "If you'd like to tell me, I'll listen."

Heather shoved out a breath and squeezed her eyes shut.

"Homicide."

Chapter Six

The word hung in the air like an icicle between them. Sharp. Jagged. Dangerous.

Shawn pursed his lips, searching for words. What was there to say?

"He killed someone." It wasn't a question, and Shawn didn't phrase it as such.

"Three people." Heather's complexion turned a pasty white. Shawn couldn't blame her. He felt a little nauseated himself. "A mother and her two children."

Oh, dear Lord, comfort her, he prayed silently. What a heavy burden Heather was carrying.

Shawn had already suspected that Heather was the victim of physical abuse, and there was no shortcut out of that camp. But the fact that Adrian had somehow killed people? That was heaping misery upon misery.

"How did it happen?" He approached the question with caution. Bringing these memories to the surface was clearly painful for Heather, but at the same time, he suspected sharing her burden with someone—with *him*—might be the first step in her healing process. He experienced a deep, burning desire to be the bridge that reconnected Heather with God and helped her find peace within herself.

"It was an automobile accident—if you can call it an accident. He ran a stop sign and sideswiped the vehicle."

"That's terrible." His chest ached so hard he thought it might burst. And if it was this bad for him, he couldn't imagine how Heather could even stand it. He wanted to do something, anything, to ease her pain. He'd never felt so helpless in all his life. His very ministry was built on his ability to come alongside people and comfort and strengthen them, guide them back to the gentle fold of God.

He searched, but he had nothing.

"It was terrible," she said, pressing her palm to her temple. "The police showing up at our door. Adrian being arrested. Finding out that children had died because of his actions. The whole thing makes me sick. And the worst part is, I was an accomplice." She swept in a breath that was half a hiccup, half a sob. "God forgive me, I let it happen."

"That can't be true." Shawn could see the shades of guilt in her gaze, but he didn't understand it. How could this sweet woman, who had done nothing to deserve the physical and emotional abuse she'd endured, blame herself for the accident? Didn't she realize that she was as much a victim as that poor family Adrian had hit?

"You see, I let him walk out the door that day. I knew he was going to get behind the wheel of a car. And he'd been—"

The doorbell rang, bringing her sentence to a grinding halt, but Shawn knew what she was about to say.

He'd been *drinking.*

This time the sharp ache in his gut was all too familiar. He knew all about alcoholism and the helplessness those who lived with such addicts felt. Surely she realized she couldn't have stopped Adrian even if she'd tried. Couldn't have stopped him from drinking, and couldn't have stopped the reckless behavior once the alcohol was in his system.

Thoughts shot through his head like bullets as he excused himself to answer the door. He wasn't expecting anyone. As he'd told Heather earlier, he rarely had visitors. He was often invited to his parishioners' homes to share a meal with them, but it was unusual for someone to come by the ranch.

Maybe someone was in the midst of a crisis. His curiosity ramped as he swung the door wide-open.

"Dad!"

"Took you long enough." The white-haired, sixtyish man with a deeply lined face and skin wrinkled beyond his years stumbled past Shawn and into the house without waiting for an invitation. "Sh-pected you'd be happy to see me, at least."

Shawn's stomach tumbled and he sent a horrified glance toward the kitchen, where Heather sat waiting for his return. Noelle was with her. The kids were playing in the backyard. This had the makings of an all-out catastrophe.

Dad's timing could not have been worse. What could he do with him to keep him from causing an unnecessary and very likely excruciating ruckus?

Shawn had been anticipating—and dreading—this confrontation with his father for a long time, but he'd never in a million years imagined circumstances like these. His father's health had been heavy on Shawn's heart for a while now, but he'd expected, or at least hoped, that he would be able to deal with this outside the watchful eyes of Serendipity.

And Heather—if she were to encounter his father...

Shawn didn't even want to know.

He took his father's shoulders and guided him toward the hallway. Maybe if he could get Dad into a back bedroom the situation would resolve itself. As soon as his father saw a bed, Shawn knew he would pass out within minutes.

"Shawn?" He heard Heather's curious voice coming from behind him and pressed harder on his father's back.

A few more feet and he could breathe easy.

He didn't anticipate his father's next move. Kenneth O'Riley planted his feet and then spun around, slipping under Shawn's grasp and staggering back toward the living room. "Didn't tell me you had company," his father cackled. "Of the female per-shway-shun."

Shawn cringed at the sound of his father's slurred words. He couldn't imagine how this episode would affect Heather—and just as he'd believed she was beginning to trust him.

Why had God let this happen? There must be a reason, but Shawn was too numb with horror to think it through.

It was bad enough that he was going to be forced into an impromptu intervention with his father, but he was far more concerned about Heather's reaction. After all, an alcoholic man had dragged her through the pit. For her to witness his father like this...

Heather rounded the corner between the kitchen and the living room, a polite, slightly strained smile on her lips. "I didn't realize you were going to have company. I'll just gather the children and leave."

Shawn scowled and stepped in front of his father, doing his best to shield Heather from seeing him. "Sounds like a plan. We'll talk later."

She wasn't buying it. Her eyes filled with curiosity, and Shawn knew why. His behavior at the moment wasn't exactly falling into the normal category as he physically blocked his father from advancing. His heartbeat pounded through his head.

Go, Heather. Please. Just go.

"Shawn?" Heather asked, her voice hesitant. "Is everything okay? Do you need me to stay?"

He met her gaze and was stunned at the strength he found there. Only moments before she'd been practically falling apart as she relayed her own horrific story, cringing away from his touch; but now she was reaching for him, gripping his forearm, offering him the support she somehow sensed he needed.

If only he could make this all go away. The

feel of her palm against his skin helped calm the panicked racing of his mind, but even as he straightened out his thoughts, he realized there was no easy way out of this mess.

"Who-sh the young lady?" his father asked with a laugh that made Shawn's hair stand on end. "Aren't sha gonna introduce us?"

Shawn's eyes met Heather's, and he shook his head almost imperceptibly. He hoped she'd understand what he meant and head for the hills.

Don't get involved. Take the kids and run.

But no. She stepped forward and offered her right hand in greeting. Her jaw was tight but her expression was resolute. She wasn't backing down.

"I'm Heather Lewis, a friend of Shawn's. And you are?"

Heather didn't have to wait for the inebriated man's answer to guess who he was. Shawn's likeness to his father was as unquestionable as the fact that the man must have started drinking near breakfast time for him to be as intoxicated as he was now.

Shawn had never said—but then, he hadn't really had the chance. Their conversation had been interrupted by the arrival of this…person.

"Kenneth O'Riley," the man said, wrapping

his clammy hand around hers and pumping it vigorously. "Sh'my pleasure."

It certainly wasn't Heather's, and it definitely wasn't Shawn's. She didn't know whether the worry lining Shawn's face had more to do with his father showing up here smashed and presumably unannounced, or whether it was because he was concerned about how she was going to handle it, but either way, she was determined to step up and come to his aid.

She could handle it. And she could help Shawn with his father.

The situation might have overwhelmed her not so long in the past, but to her astonishment, today it didn't. Maybe it was because Shawn was here with her. She knew that no matter how belligerent or out of control his father might get, Shawn would keep her safe. Perhaps it was because Shawn looked as if he was out of his element and needed her assistance.

She wasn't out of her element. Not a bit. This was home turf for her—dealing with a drunk man. Bring it on.

"Why don't you sit down, Kenneth, and I'll grab you a cup of coffee from the kitchen?" she suggested mildly, gesturing toward the couch.

Shawn nodded and clasped his father's arm, carefully leading him toward the sofa at the far end of the living room. Heather scrambled for the kitchen, taking time to check on Noelle and check on her children, who were, thankfully, still entertaining themselves throwing sticks for the Shetland sheepdog to retrieve for them. Since there were only two mugs in the house, she quickly rinsed out the one she'd been using and poured a fresh, hot cup of coffee for Kenneth. Curling her fingers around the warmth of the ceramic, she paused, closed her eyes and offered a quick prayer.

She didn't know if God would listen—not because she believed He wasn't there or couldn't be bothered, but because she wasn't worthy of approaching His throne to make requests in the first place. But she hoped for the best. After all, she was praying for Shawn, and he *was* a good, God-fearing man. Surely the Lord would hear and take account because of Shawn.

Blowing out her breath to steady her nerves, she returned to the living room and pressed the mug into Kenneth's hands. His head lolled back against the forest-green cushion, and Heather was a little worried he would spill the hot liquid into his lap.

Then again, she supposed that would get him sobered up right quick.

Shawn crouched before him and placed a hand on his knee, shaking him gently to gain his attention. "Dad. What are you doing here?"

The answer was long in coming as Kenneth attempted to focus his bleary eyes on Shawn. "Came to stay with my shon," he mumbled.

"You can't stay here. Not until you're sober. We've talked about this." Shawn's voice was gentle but firm.

Kenneth came alive, slamming his cup on the coffee table and spilling the dark liquid across the wood. "Look at this house. You're all by yourself here, and you've got plenty of room," he roared.

Shawn didn't budge, but Heather jolted backward, an instinctive and unconscious act of self-preservation. This was what she knew.

Violence.

Shawn grabbed his father's shoulder with one hand and held up the other to Heather, palm out, reassuring her that he had control of the situation.

"I'm not backing down on this, Dad. I've done some calling around and I've found a nice place in San Antonio that has an opening. They're experts. They can help you find a way out of your addiction."

Heather waited for the denial she knew was forthcoming.

"I don't see why you're pressuring me." Kenneth glared at Shawn, but to Shawn's credit, he didn't budge or capitulate. "I've said it before and I'll shay it again—you're looking at this all wrong. I'm not an alkie. I don't have to drink. I like to drink. There's a difference."

Shawn's soul-weary sigh moved the depths of Heather's heart, but Kenneth remained unfazed.

"No, Dad, that's where you're wrong. You drink to mask the pain, and until you deal with the underlying causes—David's death, Mom's illness—you will never find peace. It certainly isn't at the bottom of a bottle."

Kenneth growled in protest. "Don't you preach to me, kid. Remember who you're talking to."

Shawn shook his head. "Unfortunately, it's not something I can forget. And I'm not preaching at you. Just stating facts. Now, are you going to let me get you some help, or aren't you?"

Heather was certain no one breathed as she and Shawn awaited Kenneth's answer. For an instant the man's expression changed. He looked old, tired, weak. But then resolve took hold and Heather braced herself, hoping Shawn had also seen the subtle shift in his father's demeanor. Kenneth wasn't going down without a fight.

"I'm jush fine the way I am. Butt out of my business."

Shawn's jaw tightened and his shoulders firmed as he stood and yanked his father up with him. "Then you are no longer welcome in my house."

Heather could see the pained look in Shawn's eyes and knew just how difficult it was for him to stay strong in this. But no matter how hard it was, it was the right thing to do. She was impressed by Shawn's display of fortitude. Kenneth might be a drunk, but he was Shawn's father, and it was obvious that Shawn loved him. It was equally apparent that he refused to be an enabler—something Heather had never known how to do.

"David would never have treated me thish way," his father slurred. "You are not a good son."

Shawn winced and his expression froze. "I guess we'll never know about that, will we?" His voice was so ice-cold that Heather shivered.

Kenneth mumbled and protested as Shawn physically escorted him to the back bedroom, but Shawn was larger and stronger than his father, even without the benefit of Kenneth having had too much to drink. Shawn opened the door and deposited his father on the bed.

"Sleep it off. When you wake up, I want you to leave. You know where to find me if you change your mind." He closed the door with a firm click and turned and leaned his shoulders against it, scrubbing his hands down his face as he shoved out a breath.

"Heather, I'm so sorry for that."

"There's no need to apologize," she assured him.

"I would have told you, especially after what you've been through, but I didn't get the chance. And I certainly never expected that Dad would actually show up here in Serendipity." His shoulders slumped, the first sign of succumbing to the intense pressure he'd been under. "I don't know. I guess I should have realized it would happen eventually. He's been calling me for weeks, asking for money, mostly. I should have figured if he couldn't get at me one way, he'd try another."

"You can't anticipate what an addict will do," Heather responded, wishing there was more she could say to take the burden from him.

Their eyes met and held. His gaze was a mixture of gratitude and vulnerability, the boy he used to be dealing with his unruly father. Truly heartbreaking.

She brushed his hair out of his eyes and smoothed his temple with her fingertips as she did to soothe little Henry from his nightmares. But Shawn wasn't a child, and the action that had started as a comforting gesture transformed into a caress across his scratchy cheek. Their breath came in unison, their hearts beating as one.

He held his arms out to her. Not demanding, not forcing. Not even begging.

Just asking.

She answered by stepping into his embrace, curving her arms upward as her palms grazed the firm planes of his shoulder muscles. His hands found her waist.

For several seconds she stood immobile, working through her irrational fight-or-flight instinct, acknowledging it and letting it flow through her. Warmth and peace nudged fear out of her heart and she relaxed into his arms.

Shawn was her safe place. There was no threat here, only a man who needed the comfort of a woman's embrace and the reassurance of her words.

"You're very brave," she said.

He scoffed and leaned back so their eyes met but didn't release his hold on her waist. "Am I? Because right now I feel like a world-class jerk."

"You're not. I know it's hard now, but you did the right thing. You can't let him think he's got you fooled or he'll continue to take advantage of you. You wouldn't be doing him any favors by ignoring his addiction. At the end of the day, the best thing you can do for him is force him to see himself as he really is—locked into substance abuse. He needs to look in the mirror and understand he needs help. He's got to want it. Until that happens, there is nothing more you can do for him."

"I know." He tightened his embrace and lowered his head, his breath warm on her ear. Her heart thrummed. "But it isn't easy to say no to him. And I do wonder sometimes…" His sentence drifted into a strained silence.

"What?" she whispered when he didn't continue.

"How different things might have been if David were here."

Who was David?

The words were on the tip of her tongue to ask when they were interrupted by the clamor of children barging inside like a herd of elephants, followed by the high-pitched wail that signaled Noelle was awake.

Even though the kids were in the kitchen and couldn't see them, Shawn snapped his arms to his sides and stepped away from her. He attempted a weak smile but it didn't reach his eyes. "We're up. It sounds like our kiddos need us."

Heather regretted that the moment had passed before she could receive answers to the questions she had yet to ask. As she watched Shawn gather Noelle into his arms and shepherd the other three children toward the living room, her emotions swelled into her throat, cutting off her breath.

There was so much to learn about this man, a man whose heart was big enough to care for farm animals, a church full of people and a tiny baby girl.

He'd experienced heartache, too, and plenty of it. She'd just scratched Shawn's surface with what she'd seen today.

She wanted to know more.

Chapter Seven

Who was David?

Heather mulled over the question as she knitted a sweater for Noelle and watched her children racing from room to room playing Follow the Leader. Jacob was currently in front, and he tended to play a little rougher than his foster siblings, so Heather kept a close eye on them.

Was David Shawn's brother? And what had happened to him?

The questions haunted Heather, but despite the fact that she and the kids were now regular visitors to Shawn's ranch, she'd not been able to find an appropriate opportunity to ask. Instead, the time was spent with the children helping Shawn take care of the animals. He was a mentor and a role model for the kids, showing them how a good man thought and acted.

But he was careful never to be alone with

Heather, and he never offered any further explanation as to who David was, or what had happened to his mother that had sent his father seeking solace in a bottle. It wasn't the kind of thing one just blurted out, so she did the only thing she could do—play by his rules. He'd completely avoided talking about what had happened that day between him and Kenneth.

She understood why he didn't want to draw attention to the situation, and she didn't want to add to his sense of shame and vulnerability by bothering him about it.

She ought to just let it go—and yet she couldn't quite put it out of her mind. Whether she was playing with the children or knitting a scarf for one of the kids or answering email for a client, thoughts of Shawn would creep in. She had curiosity about his family situation, but if she was completely honest, that wasn't all there was. Her mind kept drifting to the way her emotions had skyrocketed when she was wrapped in his muscular arms.

She'd felt safe. Secure—feelings that had been foreign to her for so long. That was part of the reason why she couldn't stop thinking about it. But there was something else, something she'd never experienced before, not even when Adrian was courting her.

Her stomach tumbled with butterflies. It was

the nicest of feelings. The warm glow of a fireplace on a cold night couldn't even begin to compare.

She scoffed and returned her attention to her knitting. She was dropping stitches. And for what? Silly notions?

She needed to nip that kind of whimsical nonsense right in the bud. Even if she wasn't completely physically and emotionally scarred after Adrian, Shawn was not and could never be the man for her. He was a pastor. He had the love and respect of the entire community.

She was the beat-up, badly used and tossed-away plaything of a convicted killer. Hardly a perfect match.

A shrill scream suddenly rent the air, and Heather bolted to her feet, tossing her knitting aside. Jacob sprinted out of the hallway, his hands waving wildly and eyes wide with fright and gleaming with moisture.

"Mama, Mama, come quick," he said, grabbing her arm and urging her down the hall. "Missy hurt herself."

With her heart in her throat, Heather followed her older foster son into her bedroom, where Missy lay wailing, curled up on a pillow with her face buried in her hands. Heather's breath cut out when she heard what she immediately recognized as Missy's pain cry.

The child was really hurt.

"She hit her head," Jacob explained on a sob as Heather gathered Missy in her arms, expecting she'd need to comfort the poor little girl for getting a bump on the noggin. It wouldn't be the first time such an accident had occurred. One of the more painful lessons she'd learned as a new foster parent was that she couldn't shield her kids from all harm. Children were bound to get a few bumps and bruises along the way as they explored their world.

But when Heather rolled Missy over to pull her into the curve of her arm, she was shocked by the amount of blood covering the little girl's forehead.

Lots and lots of blood, coming from a gash that was a good half inch long and just as deep.

"Jacob, what *happened*?" she demanded, trying and failing to keep the sharp edge from her voice. It was no good panicking, and her going off would only upset the boys more than they already were. She took a deep breath and tried again. "Get me a clean towel from the linen closet, please."

Jacob dashed out and returned a moment later with a freshly bleached white towel, which Heather pressed to the wound. Poor Jacob's blue eyes were flooded with tears that ran unheeded down his face.

"It's all my fault," he wailed, clinging to Missy's hand.

"What happened?" Heather asked again in a gentler tone.

"We were jumping on your bed," he admitted miserably, not meeting her gaze.

"You know you're not allowed to—". she started, but then quickly brought her sentence up short. Jacob knew he'd broken the rules, and he was clearly distressed over what had happened to Missy. He was learning a painful lesson today and didn't need her to rub it in.

The hand towel was soaked with blood within a minute, and Heather felt a moment of panic. She was all alone with an injured child and two more who needed her care. This wasn't a scenario she'd imagined when she'd signed the papers to become a single foster mother.

She needed help. *Now.*

"Jacob, bring me my cell phone. It's on the end table next to the sofa."

He was out and back with it in a jiffy. She pressed the phone log, wondering if she had Dr. Delia Bowden's number stored. In hindsight, she realized that was something she ought to have done—put the doctor's number on speed dial. But it was too late now to rectify that oversight.

Instead, it was Shawn's number that popped

up first on the list. Not surprising. He still called nearly every day needing advice on parenting Noelle.

This time she was the one who needed *his* help. She pressed his number and waited, her breath in a knot.

He answered on the first ring. "Hey, Heather. Are you and the kids going to meet me at the ranch later to help me feed the animals?"

"Missy had an accident," she said, cutting right to the chase. "She hit her head and she's got a big gash on her forehead. I tried using direct pressure, but I can't seem to get it to stop bleeding."

"It probably needs stitches," Shawn surmised. "But don't worry, honey. Head wounds tend to bleed a lot. Doesn't necessarily mean it's serious."

"I know you're right, but it looks awful."

"I'm at the church now. Get the kids buckled up in your SUV and I'll be right there. I'll drive you to see Delia."

She breathed a sigh of relief and tears pricked at her eyes. She hadn't even had to ask for his help. She'd simply shared her problem, and that was enough to prompt him into action on her behalf.

Now was not the time to wonder why calling Shawn had been her first impulse after she realized she didn't have the doctor's number.

"Jacob, grab your coat, and get Henry's while you're at it. Just to be on the safe side, we're going to take your sister to the doctor."

The boy nodded and ran for the jackets. Heather wrapped Missy in a quilt and continued to apply direct pressure to the girl's forehead as she led the kids outside to her SUV.

"Jacob, why don't you sit in front? Pastor Shawn is coming to drive us over to the doctor's office. I'm going to sit back here with Henry and Missy, okay?"

It was only after she'd managed to get Henry buckled into his booster seat that she realized she needed to make room for Noelle, but when Shawn arrived a few moments later, he was alone.

"Where's the baby?" she asked as Shawn climbed behind the wheel.

"Jo Spencer has her. Apparently 'Auntie Jo' wants to show her off to all of her customers today."

Heather expected that statement to be accompanied by one of Shawn's frequent and heartstopping grins, so she was surprised when the corners of his lips turned down. That wasn't like him.

"How's our little patient doing?" he asked,

glancing in the rearview mirror as he started the engine.

Hmm. Maybe that was all it was. He was worried about Missy. But something niggled in the back of Heather's mind, and her gut feeling was that there was more he wasn't saying.

"It's quite a large gash. The bleeding has slowed some but it hasn't stopped yet. She'll probably have a nice scar to remember this day by."

"How'd it happen?"

"Certain little monkeys were jumping on the bed when they weren't supposed to be."

"And one fell down and bumped her head," Shawn added.

"Exactly."

"That's why you need to listen to your mama, kids," he admonished. "She knows what she's talking about, and she's trying to keep you safe."

"Now you sound like a preacher," she teased, and the back of his neck grew red. "Or a father."

He shot a look over his shoulder that Heather had a hard time identifying. Almost as if she'd— well, not insulted him, exactly, but definitely called him a name he didn't want to hear.

Which was what? *Preacher? Father?*

Nothing new there. No startling revelations. Shawn was both pastor and parent.

Shawn pulled the vehicle up in front of Delia's

office before she had the opportunity to question him about his odd reactions. He was out and around the vehicle, opening the door for her before she'd even had the opportunity to get unbuckled.

"Come on, little lady," he said, scooping Missy into his arms, careful to keep her wound covered. "Let's go see Dr. Delia and get you all patched up." He was incredibly gentle for a man his size, and once again Heather marveled at his kindness.

And she wasn't the only one who thought so. Missy gazed up at Shawn as if he were her knight in shining armor. In a way, Heather supposed he was, quick to come to their rescue when she'd called him.

Missy reached up and placed her little palm on Shawn's whisker-roughened cheek, and Heather's chest could barely restrain the swelling emotion. Such an innocent display of love and trust—and Shawn, she knew, wouldn't betray that trust. *Ever.*

Delia greeted them at the door and immediately ushered them to the back room, where she instructed Shawn to place Missy on the nearest bed. She made quick work of examining the girl. Shawn didn't leave Missy's side, and the little girl clutched his hand.

"It's not as bad as it looks," Delia assured

them. "No signs of a concussion, and the wound itself is superficial. I'll clean it up and we'll use some glue and a butterfly bandage to seal it up tight."

"I like butterflies," Missy inserted, looking hopeful.

Delia laughed. "Well, Missy, I'm afraid the bandage isn't actually a butterfly, but I'll bet I have some princess stickers around here somewhere."

Missy's excitement immediately turned to fear when Delia dabbed the wound with an alcohol swab.

"It hurts. It hurts," she wailed, fresh tears brimming in her bright green eyes.

Heather hated this part of motherhood—the part where she had to put on a brave face for her children when she was quaking inside. Shawn, however, didn't flinch.

"I know it hurts, darlin'," Shawn told the girl, pressing his palm against her cheek. He didn't try to dismiss her pain or marginalize her fear. No wonder he was such a good pastor. "You're being such a brave girl. I think cookies are called for after this, don't you? Just let Dr. Delia get you all glued up and I'll take you over to Cup O' Jo's for a treat. All of you," he added, his eyes on Jacob.

Heather wanted to hug him for including the

boy, who was still huddled in on himself in guilt. She probably would have launched herself at Shawn, if it weren't for Delia being in the room.

The doctor worked quickly, cleaning and gluing the wound, then covering it with gauze and tape. "Keep the wound clean with soap and water," she advised, "and call me if you see any signs of infection—redness around the gash or oozing from the wound. Otherwise, come back in a week for a quick follow-up."

Delia allowed each of the kids to pick out a sticker from a bucketful of choices, but she allowed Missy to have three, since the little girl couldn't choose between princesses. She liked them all, so she got them all.

Heather was relieved that Missy was all patched up and the accident had resulted in nothing more than a gash that could be fixed with a little glue. Missy seemed to have forgotten that she'd been the one on the doctor's table at all. She was the first one out the door, racing down the clapboard sidewalk with her brothers right behind her, heading toward Cup O' Jo's on the corner.

The only one who looked as if he'd been negatively impacted by the day's events was Shawn. As long as he'd been in Missy's line of sight, he'd been all smiles and strength, but now he looked as if he'd swallowed something bitter and was fighting to keep it down.

She followed Shawn out of the doctor's office and couldn't help but admire the view of the cowboy preacher replacing his straw hat and loping along after the children, but she wondered at his distracted mood. She caught up with him and laced her arm through his, half expecting resistance. He glanced at her, surprise evident in his gaze, but he slid his hand over hers and slowed to match her pace.

"No more monkeys jumping on the bed," he teased, but his attempt at a smile was faltering at best.

"Do you want to tell me what's wrong?" She applied pressure to his arm, stopping him before he could enter the café.

"I—" he started, then stopped and shook his head. "No. It's nothing. The kids are waiting for their cookies, and I'm sure Jo is plenty ready to be done with baby duty. She's had Noelle all day."

Heather highly doubted the truth of that statement. Jo Spencer loved babies above all things. She wouldn't be in any great hurry to part with darling Noelle. But Heather knew a brush-off when she heard it, so she reluctantly turned loose of his arm and allowed him to enter the café.

Jo looked up from the register when the bell

rang over the door and bustled out to greet them, her red curls bobbing with the same energy that radiated from her friendly smile. There was no sign of Noelle, but with Jo at the helm, there was no immediate cause for concern. Curiosity, perhaps, but not concern.

"Now, Pastor, I told you it wouldn't be a problem for me to drop Noelle by the church when I was finished with her."

Shawn swept off his hat and combed his fingers through his hair. "I was afraid if I waited until you tired of her you might not ever give her back. Besides, we were just down the road from here."

"We?" Jo's gaze flitted from Shawn to Heather and a wide smile spread across her face. "Ah. I see. I'm glad you two are spending time together."

Heather's face suffused with heat. Jo was jumping to all the wrong conclusions here. She'd just as much as proclaimed loud enough for half the restaurant to hear that she was seeing a couple where there were actually two single individuals with a brood of foster children between them.

"You all out for a day at the park or something?" Jo laughed as Henry pressed his nose and palms flush against the glass of the pastry case. "Looks like somebody is hungry for a cookie."

"I promised them a treat," Shawn said.

"We've just come from Dr. Delia's office," Heather explained. "Missy fell and hurt herself. Got a little gash on the head."

"Poor dear. Is she okay?"

"Delia glued the cut," Shawn said, his tone incredulous. "I didn't realize doctors don't sew you up with stitches anymore—at least not with a wound like this. Delia said she might end up with a small scar from this little incident, but three princess stickers and the promise of a cookie and I think she's forgotten her big owie already." He barked out a dry laugh. "Kids. What are you going to do with them? What kind of cookies did Phoebe bake today?"

"Chocolate with chocolate chips," Jo said, reaching in to retrieve the cookies. She removed five rather than three, and after handing out the treats to the kids, she offered the remaining cookies to Heather and Shawn. "Trust me, y'all don't want to miss these, and you two look like you could use a little pick-me-up. Chocolate cures all ills, you know."

Heather glanced at Shawn. A muscle ticked in the corner of his jaw and his mouth tightened with strain. She doubted chocolate would do anything to help what was ailing him—whatever it was.

"I'm a little remiss not to have asked where Noelle might be," Shawn said, scanning the café for his foster daughter.

Heather followed the trail of his gaze. The inside of Cup O' Jo would come as a surprise to anyone not formerly acquainted with it. The café, like all of the buildings on Main Street, had a nineteenth-century feel to its exterior, like something straight out of an old Western movie. Cup O' Jo's even boasted a hitching post out front.

But the inside of the café was a different ambiance altogether. Open and friendly, it was decorated in a contemporary, modern-coffee-shop style. Individuals hunkered over the computers lining the back walls. Several families and small groups enjoyed an early dinner. It was *the* popular spot for folks to gather in Serendipity. Chance Hawkins served up the best home-style food in Texas.

Jo threw her hands up and cackled in delight. "Why, I can't get that baby out of the back room. Chance and Phoebe are so taken with her I wouldn't be surprised if they decided it was time to start working on growing their own family again. Let me get them for you."

She hustled to the serving window and leaned

her head and shoulders into the kitchen. "Chance. Phoebe," she hollered, making Heather laugh. With Jo's voice she could have stayed right where she was. She didn't need to be at the serving window to be heard. "Pastor Shawn is here for his daughter."

It warmed Heather's heart to hear Noelle referred to as Shawn's daughter, but Shawn didn't look altogether pleased by the reference. The crease between his eyes deepened.

Phoebe, brandishing a spatula in one hand, was the first out of the kitchen. Her blue jeans and light green pullover were dusted with flour, and she had a wide streak of white on her nose, as if someone had purposefully dabbed it there. She was quickly followed by Chance, a rugged-looking cowboy with a white apron draped haphazardly around his waist. He held the baby in the crook of his arm and was murmuring nonsense to her. She clutched his thumb and kicked at her swaddling.

"She's a strong little thing," Chance said as he deposited her into her foster father's arms. "I bet she'll be a real handful when she gets a little older—and you probably don't even want to think about her teenage years. Sweet darlin'. You're gonna be needing a baseball bat to fend off all the boys."

Shawn blanched, but no one other than

Heather appeared to notice that, or the tightening of his jaw.

"It's hard to believe Aaron was ever that small," Phoebe said of her now school-aged son. "And Lucy is graduating from college this year."

"We're getting old," Chance teased, his dark eyes gleaming as he brushed Phoebe's hair in a familiar, affectionate caress.

Squealing, she wriggled away from him and wielded her spatula like a weapon. "Speak for yourself, mister. I've got a few good years in me yet."

"All right, then, I guess I'll hold off on trading you in for two twenties."

"Take that back, you!" Phoebe swatted at Chance, who easily ducked out of the way.

"Make me," he said, laughing and dodging around her.

Phoebe perched her hands on her hips. "Don't tempt me. You know I can."

Chance grinned at Shawn. "You see what I have to put up with, Pastor?" He nodded toward Heather and winked. "So much to look forward to, you know?"

"I don't see you wearing any chains around your neck forcing you to stay," Jo admonished her grinning nephew. "You wouldn't change a single thing about your life with Phoebe and you know it."

"No, ma'am, I wouldn't, and that's a fact."

"There, then, you see?" Jo crowed, delighted that the conversation had turned in her favor. "The married state is a great place to be, no question about it."

Once again, heat flared to Heather's face. Subtlety definitely wasn't one of Jo's prime virtues. Shawn's flushed cheeks signaled that he hadn't missed the not-so-delicate intimation, either.

"I've got to be going," he said, backing toward the door.

"But you came in my car," Heather protested.

"I'll walk. My truck is at the chapel, along with Noelle's car seat. See y'all in church on Sunday." He planted his hat on his head and tipped it, then was gone without another word.

"Well," said Jo as the four of them stood staring at the empty doorway.

Well, indeed. That was beyond awkward. Heather felt as if she needed to say something to explain Shawn's odd behavior, but how could she when she didn't understand it herself? Who knew what ran through a man's mind?

Clearly something was stuck in his craw. The only question was *what*?

Or maybe *who*?

Had she inadvertently done something to offend him?

The familiar sensation of panic trickled down her spine before she mindfully pressed it away. Shawn wasn't the kind of guy to react spitefully. If he had a problem with her, he would talk to her about it, not hold it over her head and leave her wondering.

As if intruding on a private moment, Chance and Phoebe awkwardly excused themselves to return to the kitchen. No doubt they felt the tension in the air, so thick a person could slice it with a knife.

Heather tried for a smile and missed the mark by a mile. "I ought to be going, as well. Let me just round up my kids and we'll be out of here. Oh." She suddenly remembered Shawn had not paid for the cookies. "How much do I owe you for the treats?"

She reached for her wallet but Jo waved her away. "Don't you dare even think about it, dear. The cookies are on me. Poor Missy deserves a little TLC after having such a scary day. Besides, my dear," she said, nodding toward the door where Shawn had just made his rather overdramatic exit, "I think you have more pressing matters to deal with."

"Yes, I certainly do." Heather didn't question why Shawn's odd behavior would be her problem. He was always there for her when she needed him, so how could she not step forward when he needed help? First, she needed to figure out what to do with her kids, and then she'd find a way to help Shawn.

"Let me feed the children a good meal for you," Jo suggested, almost as if she'd known the direction Heather's thoughts would be taking. She gave Heather a friendly pat on the back and turned her toward the door. "Go. Don't worry about your young'uns, they'll be happy as little larks here at the café. Take care of your man. I think he needs you right now."

Heather wasn't worried about her children as long as they were in Jo's care. Shawn wasn't her man, but she didn't bother to correct Jo.

Because she agreed with her on the most important point of all.

Shawn needed her.

And she would be there for him.

After leaving Cup O' Jo's, Shawn didn't bother returning home right away. It was tempting to return to the ranch. His first inclination under stress was to go out riding. Sitting in the saddle and cantering across fields was his favorite form of prayer. But he had the baby to think of, and he still had a sermon to finish, so he went back to the chapel instead.

After the great deal of excitement he imagined Noelle must have had being passed around to all his doting neighbors, he figured with a diaper change and a bottle she'd be down for the count, and he was right. In less than ten minutes the baby was sound asleep. He settled her in her car seat, which he often used to haul Noelle around with him both inside the building and in his dual-cab truck.

His unfinished sermon, scribbled on a yellow legal pad, was taunting him, but after sitting at his desk for five minutes without writing a single word, he gave up. He couldn't keep his mind on his message—he couldn't even get it there in the first place.

He needed to refocus or else he wasn't going to have two words to share with his congregation come Sunday morning. Scooping up Noelle's infant seat, he carried her into the sanctuary, where he flipped on only enough lights to illuminate the altar. He approached and knelt reverently, his gaze lingering first on the cross and then on the sleeping baby.

Had it only been a few weeks ago that this sweet little darlin' had come into his life? Right here, in this very sanctuary, his world had been forever changed. By Noelle, and by the woman who'd come to his and the baby's rescue—Heather Lewis.

He remembered how helpless he'd felt when he'd heard Noelle cry for the first time. Now that he'd been with her for a while, he could distinguish between her cries—whether she was wet, hungry or just needing a little attention.

And hurry up with that bottle, Foster Daddy.

The smile that had claimed his lips when he regarded his baby girl disappeared when he thought about the future. He'd received a troubling phone call earlier in the day, just before the one from Heather that had sent him rushing off to help the family.

The news had him all in knots. Then all that combined with the incredibly helpless feelings he'd experienced at not being able to do anything to fix Missy's injury, other than taking her to the doctor. He hated feeling as if he couldn't do anything to help.

He was a mess, and the only thing he could think of to do was to give it all to the Lord and seek His guidance. How could he lead his congregation into faith and good works if he was struggling just to plant one foot in front of the other? This was getting way beyond him. Maybe he ought to step down for a while or take a sabbatical, do a little cow-poking and spend some time on the range, under the stars.

What did God want of him?

"I'm listening," he said aloud, acknowledging his need for the Almighty.

"Good, because I'm fairly certain I have something to say."

Shawn jerked to his feet, his heart hammering. He'd thought he was alone in the chapel. He lifted his arm to shield his eyes from the glare created by the lights above the altar, but he couldn't see into the shadows.

Yet he didn't need to see to know who was there. He recognized that rich, warm feminine voice almost as well as his own.

"I didn't expect an answer," he said with a chuckle.

"No, I don't suppose you did. I'm sorry if I startled you."

"That's okay. I'll live. Did you need something, Heather? Has something happened with Missy?"

"Missy is fine. She's taking supper with the boys and Jo Spencer."

Shawn cast about for a reason Heather might be here at the church but came up empty. The only time he'd ever seen her in the chapel was the night he'd discovered Noelle. He'd gathered from talking to her that church wasn't really her thing—thanks at least in part to Adrian. So it was unlikely she'd dropped by to pray.

"The doors of the church are always open," he said, sweeping his arm out in a welcoming gesture. What else could he say?

His statement was met with a dry laugh. "Funny you should say that."

"Oh? Why?"

"I have this thing about churches. You can probably chalk it up to one of those doesn't-make-any-sense emotions, like many of the others I'm slowly working my way through. Feel free to laugh at me if you'd like."

How could he possibly make fun of her for her confusion when his own thoughts and emotions were so ruffled?

"You know I won't do that. Go on."

"It's another by-product of my time with Adrian. I'm slowly working on my own personal relationship with God, but for some reason church buildings continue to give me pause. I must have stood outside for five minutes trying to talk myself into the courage to come into the chapel tonight."

"Why?"

"Who knows? Maybe it's because attending church was absolutely the most awful experience for me when I was with Adrian. It was horrible mixing with good and honest people when my whole life was a lie. Pretending I had the perfect marriage and a charmed life, never letting on that Deacon Adrian was anyone other than the upstanding man he presented himself to be in the public light."

She shivered and crossed her arms. Shawn closed the distance between them in a second, offering her the shelter of his arms and, crazy as it might sound, desperately wishing he could protect her from the pain of her past. Wishing he could change it for her. She was defenseless against the onslaught of her memories and he couldn't step between her and her dragons. He didn't even have a sword for this fight.

She stiffened in his embrace and then relaxed into him with a sigh, clutching his shirt and resting her head on his shoulders. That alone was enough to remind him that Heather wasn't entirely at the mercy of her past experiences. She fought against them every day, but each time she took a step in the right direction she conquered more of her fears.

Whereas *he* tended to simply stuff his anxieties into the back of his mind and slam a mental door on them. He counseled people to acknowledge and work through their issues, all the while ignoring his own.

Talk about a hypocrite. She was braver than he would ever be.

"I think everyone tends to present his or her best self at church. It's natural for us to want people to like us. But let's face it—we all have issues we'd rather other folks not know about. Every one of us. What you see is never quite what you get. There aren't any truly perfect people, which is why it's such a good thing that God's mercies are new every morning."

She sniffled. "I think you come pretty close. At the very least, you're a good man if I've ever known one."

He scoffed inwardly but held his tongue. If only she knew just how wrong she was. She wouldn't be so quick to be praising him, that was for sure.

"I didn't mean to interrupt your prayer time," she said, slipping out of his arms to check on Noelle, who stirred briefly and returned to her slumber. "She's so sweet in her sleep."

"She's sweet all the time," he agreed. "And don't worry about interrupting me. I don't think I was ready to hear any answers yet. My problems are still rumbling around in my head too much. Bumping off all the rocks, you know?"

They both laughed. He was glad he could lighten the mood a little. Heather didn't look quite so uncomfortable being in the chapel now—not as she'd been when she'd first walked in. Which reminded him—she must have come here for a reason, and he had yet to find out what it was.

"I don't think you ever answered my question," he prompted. "Why'd you stop by? Is there something I can help you with?"

"Not this time," she said, sitting on the front pew, where she could easily lean over the baby. The pacifier had popped out of Noelle's mouth in her sleep and Heather gently replaced it. "I don't know how to approach what I'm about to say, so I think it's better if I just come straight out with it."

He tensed at both her words and the tone of her voice. This didn't sound good. "I value straightforwardness and honesty. Have at it."

"I want to thank you for all you've done for us today. You made a frightening situation far less so, and you are now Missy's new favorite person. You're a regular hero in her book, and in mine, too."

He scoffed and shook his head.

"Now, see, this is what I'm talking about. I know something's bothering you. Don't try to deny it. You were a total superhero with Missy, but the rest of the day? Not so much. You've been pulling back. Acting distant. Frowning when you usually smile."

"That bad, huh?" He grimaced. "I didn't think I was being so obvious."

"You cut out of Cup O' Jo's like your tail was on fire. Everybody noticed it."

Ugh. He'd hoped he'd behaved with a little more finesse than that. He slumped onto the pew next to her, pressed his face into his palms and groaned. "I got some news today."

"Bad news? I'm so sorry. If you don't want to talk about it…" Her touch was incredibly light and tender against his shoulder, but it brought him instantly alert. Even in the midst of his turmoil, or maybe *especially* in the middle of it, he was hyperaware of her proximity to him. The warmth of her breath and the soft floral scent that wafted around her. Roses.

"Not bad news, exactly, and I think you need to know about it," he replied, reaching for her hand as it drifted down his arm. He turned her palm over and brushed his lips against the spot on her wrist where her pulse beat, then threaded their fingers together. She gave his hand a reassuring squeeze. "Some of it is bad news. Some of it's good, I guess. Maybe. It could be. Or maybe not."

"You're rambling. And so far you haven't said anything."

Great. His confusion made manifest to the one woman in the world he'd most like to impress. There was danger in being this close to someone. He wanted to share his innermost thoughts and emotions, but those very same feelings made him vulnerable.

"Right. Um—" He hesitated, then plunged forward. "I got a call from Maggie Dockerty at social services. Noelle's mother has been identified."

Heather's gasp was audible. She clenched his fingers so tightly she was cutting off his circulation, but he didn't attempt to remove himself from her grasp. "That's good news, right? Or is it? What happened to her? Is she okay? Does she want to reclaim Noelle?"

He barely knew where to begin answering the questions she'd peppered him with. "Her name is Kristen Foxworthy. She was in an accident. Hit-and-run on a highway where she wasn't supposed to be walking."

"That's awful. How serious is it?"

"Unfortunately, it's very serious. She's currently in a medically induced coma, and the doctors don't give her a lot of hope. They're monitoring her brain function, which at the moment is nil. They're planning to remove the respirator. From there, I guess it's up to God what happens. It's very sad, though."

"And how do they know she's Noelle's mom?"

"Apparently she was lucid for a little while right after she was hit. She gave the emergency technicians enough information to help social services identify who was who in this case."

"So Noelle has a family, then? Someone who might want to take her?"

"Not that they can find. They think that's

why Kristen was wandering the streets, poor girl. She must have been devastated—and desperate—to leave Noelle the way she did. I've been praying for her nonstop. I guess that's all we can really do."

"Yes. We should pray," Heather agreed, her voice breaking. "That's probably most important. Are you going to go see her?"

Shawn's gaze shot to hers. She looked back at him with a clear and determined focus he'd not seen before.

With faith.

"Yes. I'm planning on it."

"I thought you might. Where does that leave Noelle?"

"Right now? Nothing's changed. But when they take Kristen off the ventilator…well, she's not expected to make it."

"Then Noelle becomes a ward of the state."

"Yes."

"And then you can officially adopt her." Heather's voice built in volume along with her excitement. "You'll be able to give her a permanent home. Watch her grow up."

"That's just it. I'm not sure I'm going to be able to do that. The whole adoption thing—I've been thinking about it since the day Noelle entered my life, and I don't believe I'm cut out for it. I mean, I've wondered, you know, if I could be a father."

"What do you mean *if* you could be a father? Of course you could. You *are*. You're doing a great job with her. You've adapted to being a daddy a lot better than many of the natural fathers I know."

"I won't be enough for her. I grew up with only my dad watching over me. My mom, she—" He paused a beat. "She was out of the picture."

He didn't think it was necessary to add that his dad hadn't been much of a father. Heather had met the man and seen him in action. Kenneth O'Riley was an addict. His affection had been misplaced. Shawn had had nothing positive to draw on, no role model to grow up with.

And that was before even considering what Shawn himself had done—or failed to do, with David. Was it fair or safe to put Noelle into his care permanently?

"That must have been rough for you."

"I'm not looking for sympathy. It was what it was, and anyway, I deserved it. But even if there wasn't my lack of background in good family dynamics, I'd still worry that I'm not suited to parenthood. Today with Missy solidified it for me."

"I'm not following. You were wonderful with Missy."

"Maybe on the outside it seemed that way. Inside my gut was turning over like a combine and I thought my heart was going to beat out of my chest. What I mean is—well, I don't want to freak you out or anything, but what if her injury had been worse? What if I had made the wrong decision and she'd ended up in serious trouble? I didn't know whether we should have called the paramedics. I made assumptions when I probably shouldn't have. I'm no expert."

"It could have been worse," Heather acknowledged. "But it wasn't."

"And then I thought about Noelle, and what would happen if I adopted her. Something bad could happen to her and I would be powerless to stop it. And what if I made the wrong decision in the aftermath, and made things worse? I don't think I could handle it if something serious happened to one of these kids. Yours or mine."

"Do you hear yourself? That's an incredibly defeatist attitude—and coming from you. You've jumped off the bull before it's even out of the gate."

"I know it seems that way, but—"

"But what, Shawn? Help me to understand. I see your reluctance. Feel it, even. It's no small commitment you and I are considering, and our circumstances are far from ideal. It's only natural that we'd be scared of the responsibility. But at the end of the day, we aren't really in control of anything, are we? We don't know what is going to happen from moment to moment. Every breath is a gift. Some of what happens to us and to the kids is going to be bad. Yes. But some of it will be good. Really good."

She gestured to the sleeping infant. "Remember that amazing feeling you had the first time this sweet baby girl smiled at you? Well, there's more to come. She'll take her first step. It'll happen before you know it. And she'll say her first word, which I can tell you right now is going to be *Dada*."

He grimaced.

She smiled. "I don't know about you, but I accept the bad things that have happened to me. I hate that they happened, and I don't know that I'll ever completely recover. But those circumstances led me to having the heart to foster Jacob, Missy and Henry, and I wouldn't miss that for the world."

"You're thinking of adopting them?"

"More than thinking about it. I've started filling out the paperwork. These kids have become everything to me—and I can't imagine my life without them."

She absently rubbed her thumb over his. He thought she probably wasn't even aware of the motion, but for him, it was as if his skin had grown millions of little nerve endings, each one full of electricity.

"I know it's not the traditional way of things. Us being single parents depending on help from friends and the community rather than spouses and family. And I do want the best for them. But these kids…" Her voice broke. "If they didn't have me, they'd have no one."

"They deserve you. And you deserve them. Don't ever doubt yourself. I'm happy for you."

"But that's not how it's going to be for you and Noelle." It was a statement and not a question, and although he was certain Heather didn't mean it that way, it almost felt like an accusation. It was the dark shadow of his own guilt lingering over him.

"No, I don't think it is." He could barely get the words out from between his clenched teeth, but it was all he could do to control the emotions thundering through him like a herd of wild horses—anger, shame, guilt, longing.

"Is it because of your pastorate? Are you afraid you won't have enough quality time to spend with her? You know the people of Serendipity are going to gather around you and support you. Noelle will have more female role models than she knows what to do with. She'll have me."

"I know—you're right about that. And I appreciate that you'd be there for Noelle. But I just can't be responsible for another human life."

"What did you say? Another?"

"That's right." His gaze met Heather's and time stopped. He forgot to breathe. How quickly her curiosity would turn to aversion once he told her about David. But it was time for her to know the truth. "I was responsible for my brother's death."

Chapter Eight

"David." Heather hoped her voice didn't waver. Her mouth had suddenly gone as dry as the Texas plain in the middle of summer. It was all coming together. She could now make an educated guess as to who David was, and she wished she couldn't. She wasn't sure she wanted to hear Shawn's next words.

His face said it all.

"How do you know about David?"

"I don't, really. I heard you talking about him when you were speaking with your father, but I had no idea he was your brother until now. What happened?"

She clung to his hand. Whatever he was about to say, she wanted him to know that she still believed in him. Cared for him, more than she wanted to admit, and definitely more than she should.

"I was eight years old, just a little bit younger than Jacob, and David was six," he began, his lips quirking with anguish at the memory. "We were on vacation. At the beach off the coast of California. It's the only time I've ever been to the ocean. Before or since."

His eyes took on a faraway look, and she knew he was seeing the moment as if it were happening again. She wanted to put her arms around him but feared that might be too much for him. She knew how it felt to need to get something out without drowning in emotion. So she did the best thing she knew how to do. She listened.

"We were playing in the waves. My brother, he had this Irish complexion. As ginger as they came. You know—bright red hair, fair skin, freckles. The sun was roasting him as red as a cherry. Mom forgot to bring the sunblock out to the sand, so she sent us back to the car to get the bottle."

He groaned and shook his head, his fingers biting into her palm.

"I was only distracted for a second. There was this sand crab on its back. I was watching it struggle to turn over."

"Sounds like something any eight-year-old boy would be doing." She tried not to tense, knowing he would feel her stiffen, but her pulse was beating rapidly as her mind filled in the blanks. Even without all the details, she knew what was coming. Her stomach lurched.

"I unlocked the car door and David crawled into the backseat, digging for the lotion in one of Mom's canvas swim bags. I threw the keys on the front seat, Heather. I don't know why I did that. How stupid could I be?"

His voice broke and his gaze broke away from hers. His struggle was evident in his rigid jaw and the tense lines of his neck.

She wanted to tell him it was all right, but of course it wasn't, and would never be. She was afraid if she spoke she'd only make things worse for him. So she waited, silent, for him to finish his tragic story.

"He was goofing around, pretending to drive. Pushing all of the buttons and pulling at the wheel. I yelled at him to knock it off but he wouldn't listen to me. I kept thinking of how Mom was going to be mad at me for letting David push the buttons, like maybe when she started the car and the windshield wipers would go on or something."

"It wasn't the wipers you had to worry about," she guessed.

"No," he growled, agonized and angry. "It

wasn't the wipers. Or the air conditioner. Or anything else on the dashboard. He hit the door lock."

"Goodness," Heather said in a breathy voice, hardly able to absorb the incredibly tragic story. And to think Shawn had carried it around on his shoulders all these years. Her heart ached for him.

"It was so hot that day. I didn't know what to do. I didn't realize how quickly hyperthermia could set in."

"Of course you didn't. You were only eight."

"He begged me to help him." Shawn's face turned as white as his shirt. "He screamed for me. I didn't know what to do. I tried to talk him through it, to get him to unlock the door, but he didn't understand what I was trying to tell him. All of those buttons. I couldn't get him to push the one that unlocked the car."

Heather was so deep in her own imagination, picturing the event, that she nearly started out of her skin when Noelle let out a wail. Shawn immediately disengaged from Heather, jamming his fingers through his hair, clearly as dazed as she was. But she intensely missed his touch when he walked away from her.

Glad to have something constructive to do, she scooped Noelle into her arms, shushing her mildly and rocking her back and forth. She wished it was as easy to comfort Shawn in his grief.

"David was rapidly overheating," Shawn continued. "I didn't know all the ins and outs of what was happening to him, but I could see the changes in his face. I can still see him staring at me, terrified, his palms pressed against the glass. I was his big brother. He depended on me to save him, and I couldn't. Lord forgive me, but I couldn't."

"It's not your fault, Shawn. It was a terrible accident, to be sure, but you weren't the cause of it."

"No, maybe not directly, but I could have stopped it from happening. I should have been more careful. I should have held on to the keys and put them in my pocket instead of throwing them on the seat of the car. I shouldn't have gotten distracted with that stupid crab. I should have recognized how serious the circumstances were as soon as I realized he'd locked himself in the car. Maybe if I'd run for my mother straightaway things might have turned out differently. By the time I comprehended that I needed adult help, it was too late for David."

"Could the adults have done anything to save David if you'd brought them in earlier, do you think? Your mom, I mean? Did she have an extra set of keys? What could she have done in that short space of time that you didn't do?"

"I don't know. I don't know." He slumped back onto the pew and covered his face in his hands.

"Then how are you at fault? Explain that to me?" She hated to push him, but she needed him to see the truth—that it was a terrible accident for which no one was to blame.

"Do you know what David's death did to my mom? She's institutionalized, Heather. She completely lost her mind thanks to me. She needs psychotic meds and constant supervision just to make it through the day, even all these years later."

He scoffed in disgust. "You want to know why my dad drinks so much? Well, there you have it. Because of me."

The hard edge to Shawn's voice upset Noelle, who protested and squirmed in Heather's arms. The baby wasn't used to having her daddy use that tone of voice.

Heather thought Shawn was lost in his own world, but he immediately noticed how his reaction had affected his baby.

"I'm upsetting her." He held his hands out and Heather transferred Noelle into his arms. "I'm sorry, little darlin'. It's all right. I'm here, baby. Nothing's going to hurt you while I'm around."

Heather wished Shawn could see himself through her eyes. She wanted him to see what she saw—a man who had beat nearly insurmountable odds to become a pastor. He'd spent his life helping other people and didn't think twice about putting his own convenience on the line for the sake of the abandoned baby girl.

Most men would have passed Noelle off to the system. But not Shawn. He'd given the baby his very best. He gave everyone his very best. And it *was* enough, even if he couldn't see it right now.

"I still see David's face when I close my eyes," he continued in a soft, carefully modulated tone of voice. "Forever reaching out to me. Calling for help. Not only in the daytime, either. I have nightmares."

"I know where you're coming from with the nightmares. Not a night goes by that I don't wake up drenched in a cold sweat."

Even in the midst of his own turmoil, Shawn's gaze flooded with compassion. "Because of what Adrian did to you."

"No," she countered in surprise. "I mean, I suppose I still think about that sometimes, but my nightmares are of the family Adrian hit with his car, the children I could not save."

Shawn grunted and shook his head. "You can't blame yourself for what happened. That was all on Adrian."

"But looking back on it, I feel like I could have stopped him from walking out the door in the first place. I should have tried harder. I knew he was drunk, and I knew he was going to climb behind the wheel. Hindsight is twenty-twenty. Like with you throwing the car keys on the seat instead of putting them in your pocket. We can't stop the regrets over the things we'd do differently if we had the chance to do it all again."

"But there aren't any do-overs in life."

"No. No, there aren't. There's no going back. But we *can* move forward, and that's where I think you've got it all wrong."

Shawn stiffened. The woman certainly didn't mince words. She didn't hesitate to point out that he was wallowing in his own misery. If he was being brutally honest with himself, he had been wallowing for years.

And Heather was calling him on it.

Resentment built for exactly one second before he took in Heather's demanding hazel-eyed gaze, challenging him to push his pride aside. His respect for her grew with every beat of his heart. Every time he was with her, he grew to appreciate her more.

Respect, appreciation and…something more. If things were different for him—for them—he might have pursued that line of thought. But circumstances being what they were, he consciously pushed his feelings aside. Heather had just said she was in the process of permanently adopting her three kids. She didn't need him and Noelle to further complicate her life.

"Would you answer a question honestly if I asked you to?" she asked.

"I'm always honest, but whether I answer or not depends on the question."

"The day we were in San Antonio. You were prepared to hand Noelle over to the state, and then suddenly you weren't. Why not? What changed?"

"That's two questions." Shawn laughed, trying to shake off the tension between his shoulder blades, but it remained, fierce and tight.

"I don't know. I guess I had it in my mind that she'd be going straight into a loving home."

"Mom, dad, two-point-five kids, a dog and a white picket fence?"

She got him. Again.

He quirked his lips. "Something like that."

"But?"

"But the reality was sobering. I hadn't realized that Noelle was probably going to end up in a state home, at least at first. I know after I got her tested that she was negative for drugs, but who knows what would have happened if she'd become a ward of the state. They might have labeled her a possible drug baby even before the testing, which would mean she'd never get a fair shot. Or—well, I don't know where she might have landed."

"And you still don't. That's the real point here, isn't it? You *didn't* know where she would end up and so you stepped up to make sure she had a soft, safe landing."

"I suppose. I didn't have a lot of time to think about it. It was more a reaction than an action."

Heather smiled, and Shawn's heart jumped into his throat. She stroked his arm where Noelle was cradled and sleeping, and then she shoved out a breath.

"Now, Pastor Shawn O'Riley, you have the opportunity to change that reaction into an action. A very important, thoughtful and loving action."

"That's what *you're* going to do, isn't it? Adopt your kids?"

"Yes, I'm going to try. When I originally agreed to foster my three, I was driven by a sense of guilt over the children Adrian killed, but now…"

"Now it's all about love." He could see it in her eyes, hear it in her voice. Even the rose-laced scent of spring in her perfume hinted at new beginnings.

He wanted that. He wanted what she had. She carried this deep, abiding assurance that she was doing the right thing. And it hadn't come easy to her. He knew how hard she'd worked for it, how much she'd overcome, and that only made him want it more.

He had every confidence that Heather would succeed with whatever she put her mind to, up to and including adopting her three children. He just didn't know if it was possible for him to do the same.

He settled Noelle back in her car seat and buckled her in. Heather reached for his elbow and turned him around.

"Promise me you'll think about it, at least," she whispered. "That you won't make any rash decisions without talking to me first."

He couldn't help but doubt himself, although seeing Heather's courage in the face of conflict somehow infused his spirit with a new energy. And when he looked into her eyes, he saw what she'd been trying to say all along but that his ears and his stubborn heart refused to hear.

She believed in him.

It was right in front of him—her faith, her strength, her hope for the future, and...

His entire being warmed with what he saw in her gaze. It wasn't that he'd never thought about this—he had. Many times. But she had so many emotional walls up, and rightly so, that he'd never considered it might actually come to pass.

He never thought... He never imagined that he might be the man to break down those barriers. He'd put up his own walls as well, but the second he looked into her eyes, he forgot what they were.

He didn't move. Didn't breathe, even. Didn't want to be the one to ruin this moment with a misplaced word or wrong movement.

She was the one who closed the distance between them. She stepped forward and reached for his hands, wrapping them around her waist, and then she laid a tentative hand on his jaw. It was the lightest of caresses, but he was a goner. Shawn leaned into her touch. His gaze dropped to her full lips. She was smiling as she tilted her head up to his.

"Heather, I—" he started, but she brushed a finger across his mouth, silencing him before he could continue.

"Please, Shawn. No words. Just please—kiss me."

His heart slammed into his ribs and it took

every bit of his self-control for him not to do just that. There was nothing in the world he wanted so much as to taste her lips and drink in the strength and tenderness of this wonderful, magnificent woman.

But he had to be sure—that she was sure. He was caught up in the moment, and she might be, too. If she was, she might not really be ready, and she might not know how to put the brakes on. He couldn't begin to imagine everything she'd been through, and so he didn't know quite how to proceed.

"There are only two people in this room right now," she said, the timbre of her voice a low purr. She clutched his shirt and pulled him forward, closing whatever distance had been left between them. "Well, except for the baby, and she's asleep."

She chuckled against his lips. It was the laughter that relieved Shawn of any anxiety he was feeling.

He kissed her slowly but thoroughly, softly exploring every inch of her lips. He let her set the pace while he simply reveled in her—her touch, her taste, the smell of roses.

This woman was meant to be cherished, honored and loved by a man with his whole heart. She was all that was good and right in the world, and the fact that she had chosen him, at least for today, that it was *his* arms she'd allowed to shelter her, made him feel honored and blessed, as well.

And when she sighed and deepened the kiss, time stood still.

Chapter Nine

Heather opened the hatch to her silver SUV and let Will Davenport handle loading her groceries so she could concentrate on getting the children buckled into their seats. Sam's Grocery was located on the corner of Main Street with a designated lot in the back for the customers to park. And fortunately for Heather, it also provided a handsome ex-military man who was married to the owner and guaranteed her customers got first-class service.

Getting personalized assistance was one of the perks of small-town Serendipity that Heather liked and appreciated—the special service at Sam's Grocery, for example, where her groceries were not only bagged for her but toted to the car, making shopping that much less of a hassle, especially when she had the children with her.

"Thank you so much, Will," she said out the

window when he tapped her hood in the universal sign for "good to go."

"My pleasure, Heather. We'll see you next week."

Heather glanced at her reflection in the rearview mirror and smiled softly. Little did Will and his wife, Samantha, know they would be seeing her sooner than that. She was planning to shock everyone—herself most of all—when she attended church on Sunday morning.

It was high time her children started Sunday school, especially since she now intended for them to stay in Serendipity on a permanent basis. It was her new opinion that every child should be brought up in a church—as long as it was the kind of church pastored by a man like Shawn O'Riley.

She touched her lips, remembering the tender way he'd kissed her. In the chapel, of all places—which might have been shocking were it not so sweet. They'd been interrupted by Noelle's fussing before long, anyway.

Her heart flared to life every time she thought about his lips on hers—thoughts that had occurred with striking regularity in the two days since she'd last seen him. But doubt quickly extinguished the flames.

When she'd kissed Shawn, she'd been absolutely, 100 percent certain of what she was doing. She would not have approached him otherwise. In the years since her divorce, she hadn't had the least bit of desire to be held by a man, much less be kissed by anyone. If anything, she was revolted by the mere thought of it. And yet with Shawn it was different.

With him, everything was different.

She was a little embarrassed at the enthusiasm with which she'd initiated that particular string of events. It was so…*forward*. Especially for her.

And it wasn't as if she'd missed the fact that he'd hesitated.

More than once.

The more often she replayed the scene in her mind, the clearer it became. He'd verbally tried to stop her, or at least slow her down, but she hadn't even let him speak. She'd quite literally thrown herself at him, taking his arms and placing them around her waist. He hadn't fought it, but she wasn't sure he would have taken that step on his own.

She'd so desperately wanted to feel his strength that she'd given no thought to the awkward position she'd placed him in—or the awkwardness she herself would face in the aftermath. Her cheeks heated with shame even thinking about it.

What must he think of her?

She didn't know for certain, but it didn't take a rocket scientist to speculate on the issue. He hadn't called her in two days. He was probably avoiding her.

Granted, she hadn't tried to get in touch with him, either, but it wasn't because she didn't want to see him. Quite the opposite, in fact.

There was no going back for her. All she wanted in the world was to step right back into the warmth and safety of his strong arms and feel the tenderness of his embrace. But she'd already made a fool of herself once. She was in no hurry to repeat the humiliating ordeal.

The confidence that had propelled her into Shawn's arms had faded quickly once the kiss was over, replaced by her usual insecurities. Was she fooling herself to believe she and Shawn might have a future together? Was it even fair of her to ask him to take her on, given his lack of confidence in his parenting ability and her commitment to her children?

Better to give them both some room. Let the air cool between them.

"Mama, you drive?" Henry asked from the backseat.

Heather laughed. "I suppose I ought to be driving, since we're sitting here in the car and all. We'd best get home and unload these groceries."

She turned the key in the ignition and took

another quick glance in the rearview mirror before backing out of her parking space.

She didn't know why she noticed the man parked at the far end of the lot, leaning on a nondescript white sedan.

A subtle movement, perhaps? Leftover survival instinct?

Despite his shaggy hair and unkempt beard, Heather immediately recognized him. Cold blue eyes turned her stomach. Lightning flashed before her eyes, thunder rumbled in her chest and her breath twisted as if caught up by gale-force winds.

"Oh, God, save us," she whispered, her words very much a prayer. She ducked out of sight before she'd given it a second thought.

Adrian.

What was he doing in Serendipity? He was supposed to be in jail.

Had he seen her? Recognized her? How had he found her? A lucky guess that she'd gone back to her hometown?

He'd probably seen her. He'd appeared to be looking right at her when she'd spotted him.

What to do? What to do?

The children. She'd inadvertently put them in danger. If they were with her, Adrian could harm them.

She had a permanent restraining order against

him. Technically, he wasn't legally allowed to get as close to her as Sam's small parking lot afforded. But a restraining order was nothing more than a piece of paper when it came to an angry, drunken man. Adrian had never been much for following the law even before he'd gone to prison, and she had no reason to believe he'd do so now.

She locked the doors and scrambled to locate the cell phone in her purse, all without lifting her head above the height of the dash.

"Kids, we're going to play a little game right now," she said, trying to keep her voice calm and steady. She closed her hand around the phone and hiccuped in relief. "Everyone duck down in your seat until I say 'peekaboo.'"

"What's wrong?" Jacob asked, ever astute and sounding slightly offended. He was too old to be playing peekaboo with his mother.

"Please, Jacob, just do as I say. I'll explain when I can."

Her breath lodged in her throat and her heart hammered as she dialed 911 and waited for the operator to pick up.

What if Adrian approached the vehicle? How would she keep the kids safe? She didn't dare even spare a backward glance to see if he was coming toward her. If somehow by the grace of

God he hadn't already seen her, she didn't want to accidentally tip him off.

"What is the nature of your emergency?"

"I think I'm being followed. My ex-husband is out of prison. I have a permanent restraining order against him but I don't feel safe."

"What is your location?"

"Sam's Grocery. The parking lot. I'm in a silver SUV. I have my three children with me. Please hurry."

"A unit has already been dispatched. ETA less than a minute."

Another reason to be grateful for small towns. But a lot could happen in a minute.

"Mom?" Jacob spoke again. "Who is following us? Did you just call the cops?"

"Yes, honey, and they are on their way to help us. I'll explain it all to you, I promise, but right now we need to stay low and wait for the police to get here."

She jumped when someone rapped on the driver's-side window but was relieved to see Slade McKenna nodding at her. She'd never been happier to see red and blue flashing lights.

She rolled the window down a crack. "Slade. Thank you for coming so fast."

"Where did you see your ex-husband?" Slade cut straight to the chase with no formalities.

"He's directly behind me, at the far end of

the lot. Blond hair. Beard. He's driving a white sedan, although he was out of the vehicle when I saw him."

Slade glanced in the direction she indicated and frowned. "Keep your doors locked and your head down. Stay right where you are until I return."

Tension crackled through the air as Heather counted every heartbeat. Her own breath sounded painfully loud. In what seemed like hours later but was probably only a matter of minutes, Slade returned and once more tapped on her window.

He pressed his lips together before speaking. "I'm sorry, Heather, but there's no sign of him."

"What? No," she disputed, regaining her seat and turning to look over her shoulder. "He's right—"

But the space where the white sedan had been parked was empty. She scanned the lot, hoping to point him out so the police officer could arrest him, but Slade was correct.

Adrian was gone.

Had she been seeing things? The Adrian she knew had always taken great pride in his clean-cut appearance. It was one of the ways he fooled everyone. But the man she had seen, unkempt and bedraggled, had looked every bit the criminal he was, and for that reason was that much more intimidating.

No, she wasn't mistaken. She'd seen him. And if he'd seen her, then not only her safety but the safety of her children was at stake. How could she ever possibly have thought of adopting these precious children and putting them in danger?

"I didn't imagine him." She couldn't have.

"No, of course not, Heather. I totally believe you. He was here. I've radioed the station and put out an APB on the guy. He's not going to get very far. We've got all our eyes watching for him. And we have a patrol car scheduled to run down your block on an expedited basis, okay?"

That Slade believed her—that the *police* believed her—gave her a measure of comfort but no real confidence. Adrian was a smart man. If he wanted to confront her, he'd find a way to do it. He'd get around the police somehow.

"I'm sorry I couldn't nab the guy for you today. Is there anything else I can do for you? Just name it."

"I appreciate your help, Slade, and there's no need to apologize. You got here as fast as you could." Other than assigning her a 24/7 police escort, which was completely beyond the scope of Serendipity's police department, there was little Slade could do.

Or maybe there *was* something. "There is one

thing. Is there any way for you to find out when and why he was released from prison? I thought he still had at least a few more years to serve before he'd be eligible for parole, which is why I was doubly shocked to spot him here."

"Where was he imprisoned?"

"Colorado."

"I'll get that information to you right away. We'll pick him up as soon as we see him and get him locked back up again. He's already violated your restraining order, and if he's out of a prison in Colorado, it's a good bet he's broken his parole."

If they caught up with him. *If* they could catch him.

Those were pretty big *ifs*.

Adrian had contested their divorce when she'd filed, but there was little he could do about it from prison. She hadn't wanted anything from him and she hadn't taken anything other than her clothes and what was left of her dignity.

He was frightening when he was angry. And if he was here—in violation of his parole and his restraining order—then he was angry.

But she wasn't the same woman Adrian had intimidated for all those years. She had found a renewed sense of strength, hope and faith, thanks in large part to her relationship with Shawn.

All the angst and awkwardness she'd been

feeling earlier over their kiss dissolved with the gravity of these new circumstances. She had some serious decisions to make about her life, and there was one person in this world who'd had a real glimpse of the depths of her heart, one man who would truly understand what Adrian's abrupt arrival in her life meant for her and the children.

Already more than halfway home, she turned her car around and headed for Shawn's ranch.

Shawn had picked up his phone to call Heather at least a dozen times in the two days since they'd had their *moment* and he'd replaced the phone without actually making the call every time.

He'd never been in this position before. He'd never expected he would come to feel the way he did about Heather, and he didn't want to scare her off with the intensity of his emotions. And the worst of it was that he wasn't sure he could mask how he felt. And even if he could, he still wasn't certain he would be able to step up and be the man Heather needed him to be.

He did what he always did when he needed to think—went out to the barn to tend the animals. He might not talk out loud to them the way Heather had done in her youth, but there was a certain amount of comfort in the routine of pitching hay and even in mucking the stalls. No-elle seemed to like being strapped to his chest and contentedly watched what he was doing.

At least he was learning how to please one of the women in his life.

How was he supposed to hide his feelings for Heather when he wanted to shout them from the mountaintop? If he had his way, he'd scoop her clear off her feet, swing her around and laugh and hug and sing.

Well, okay, maybe not sing. He didn't want to send her off screaming with her hands over her ears.

Heather had done such a number on him that he felt as if he were floating. Walking on clouds. Who knew that all those overly romanticized stories about falling in love were actually true?

Kissing Heather—now that was a game changer.

For him, at least.

For her? He couldn't begin to guess.

She'd taken his hand and pulled him through his past, helped him to finally acknowledge all that had happened. Hopefully he would finally be able to start working through it. The problem was, he didn't know how to perceive the kiss that had followed that wonderful talk. She was such a generous and compassionate woman. Was that why she'd kissed him? Had she just so completely empathized with his situation that she'd got caught up in that whirlwind?

She'd certainly given him enough food for thought where permanently adopting Noelle was concerned—and she'd made him promise not to make any rash decisions. Nothing compared to a good woman challenging a man to step up and face adversity head-on. He was definitely thinking about it now, opening his mind to the possibilities of the future.

All the possibilities. He just didn't quite know what his life would look like yet. He felt as if he were on the verge of a discovery that hovered just out of his reach. There were blank spaces he had yet to fill in.

The sound of car tires crunching on the gravel in his driveway not only surprised him, but also gave him a moment's hesitation. He wasn't expecting anyone, and the last time he'd had an unanticipated visitor, it had been his father.

Just what he didn't want to deal with today.

Steeling himself for the worst, he tossed one last pitchfork of hay into the nearest horse's stall, shifted Noelle to fit more firmly against his chest, adjusted his hat lower on his brow and exited the barn. If it was his dad, it was better just to get the confrontation over with.

But it wasn't his father's beat-up vehicle that

had pulled up in front of his house. It was Heather's SUV, and she had all her kids with her.

He didn't care that she'd come unannounced. In fact, he was relieved. If she was here then she wanted to see him. And if she wanted to see him...

A smile split his face and his pulse burst to life, and he knew exactly why. He was seeing his favorite people. Heather and her children made his life here on the ranch complete.

He'd been trying to fill in the blanks in his life, but until he saw Heather, he hadn't realized that the missing pieces of the puzzle were the people who'd come to mean more to him than anything in the world.

He rushed forward to open the door for Heather, trying not to give away the gymnastic backflips his heart was currently performing. He wanted to tell her everything he'd learned about himself—and how he felt about her—but this wasn't the right time or place. They had their little tribe with them right now, and that was what was important.

The right time would come. He just knew it.

His smile widened even more, if that were possible. His whole world was opening up. It was as if the day had suddenly dawned on him and he could see everything around him, crystal-clear and sparkling.

Until he saw Heather's face.

She wasn't smiling. Her eyes were glassy and red. Her complexion had faded to a pasty white. And she was visibly shaking.

The ground dropped from under him as he reached out his arms to steady her. "Heather, honey, what's wrong?"

Her lips thinned and she shook her head. "Not here."

The children. Of course. Whatever was bothering her, she didn't want to share it with the kids around to hear.

He opened the back door and unbuckled Henry while Heather used the opposite door for Jacob and Missy. With his heart in his throat, Shawn herded the three out to the back to play with Queenie, and then he settled Noelle in her crib. Thankfully, she was sound asleep and probably wouldn't waken from her nap for a while.

He wasn't sure he wanted to hear what Heather had to say. Both grief and determination were evident in her gaze, and she hadn't yet said a word.

This was serious.

He joined her in the kitchen and poured each of them a cup of coffee, and then slid onto the chair opposite her. Neither one of them spoke, and tension was thick in the air between them.

She was unhappy. It sliced his heart into tiny pieces to see her this way. Especially if he was the cause of it.

Maybe she was trying to figure out a way to let him down easy. Had she spent the past two days wondering how to gently tell him to take a hike?

He couldn't stand to see her this way. He wanted to reach out to her, to thread his fingers with hers, but he was afraid that would be exactly the wrong thing to do in these circumstances—whatever they were.

He should just make it easy for her.

"About the other day..." he started, then stopped and tried to clear the huskiness from his throat. How did a man apologize for a moment that he considered one of the best in his life?

"I saw Adrian."

Her declaration hung in the air for a beat and then plunged into his lungs and gutted his rib cage.

"What did you say?" He must have heard her wrong. "I thought Adrian was in prison—for a long time yet to come."

"Yes, well, evidently not." Her voice was laced with sarcasm, anxiety and, above all, anger.

"Tell me." Shawn didn't think twice about reaching across the table and taking her hand. Not now. Her fingers clung to his like a lifeline.

She related the story of how she'd seen Adrian in the parking lot of Sam's Grocery. How he'd been staring straight at her but hadn't approached. How she'd called the police but the man had disappeared.

How she knew he'd be back.

Shawn's determination to protect her grew with every word she spoke. If this Adrian guy thought he was going to stalk Heather or intimidate her—or worse—he had another think coming.

Shawn wasn't about to let Adrian anywhere near the woman he loved.

"Why do you think he's here?" Cold settled into Shawn's gut and the muscles across his shoulders tightened. With the amount of adrenaline pumping through him, he hoped she wouldn't feel him quiver.

"Honestly, I have no idea. I didn't think he'd be out of prison so soon. It's in his best interest to stay as far away from me as possible."

"You'd think."

"But he's not. Which means he's got a real problem with me. Who knows what a man in that state of mind might do? He's already broken his permanent restraining order, and probably violated his parole, as well. I requested advanced warning for his parole hearings, but somehow I didn't receive that notice. Maybe there was a glitch in the prison system. And the most frightening part of this whole experience was that I had the kids with me in the car. To think that their being with me might put them in any danger— It makes me sick to my stomach."

She wasn't the only one feeling that way. Shawn's gut was roiling.

"What are the police doing about it?"

"Everything they can. Slade said they put out an APB on him, and I was able to give them quite a bit of information as to what they're looking for. They're scheduling a patrol car to run by my house on a regular basis. If they see him and pick him up, he's going straight back to jail."

"That's not good enough." Shawn shook his head vehemently. "You and the kids aren't safe as long as that guy is lurking around."

"No," she agreed. "We'll never really be safe. Not ever. I thought after the divorce I wouldn't have to see Adrian again, but now I realize I'll never be rid of him. Even if they send him back to prison, he'll eventually get out again. Everything has changed now."

For the worse.

Shawn wasn't about to let Heather lose everything she'd worked so hard to gain.

"I can't have someone watching over me 24/7, so I'm really out of options. I feel like I ought to hold off on signing those adoption papers." Her hazel eyes flooded with tears. "He's going to be a permanent nightmare for me."

Adrian's threat would haunt her for the rest of her life.

Shawn couldn't let that happen.

"There's another way."

The revelation didn't dawn on Shawn—it knocked him over. The solution was simple. Right before his eyes.

"Yeah? What's that?" She sounded unconvinced, but he supposed he would, too, if he were in her position.

"Marry me."

"What?" She practically choked on the word.

"Marry me," he said again, emphasizing each syllable.

She made a sound halfway between a chuckle and a sob. "Nice try, mister. Thank you for your attempt to lighten the mood."

Lighten the mood? Did he not look serious?

She wasn't getting it. For a man who communicated for a living, he was doing a poor job of it. Marrying him would fix everything. He had to make her see that.

He stood and moved around the table without releasing her hand. He didn't want anything between them. Not now. He wanted to be near her, to touch her and make her believe. He took a seat in the chair next to her and placed her palm on his chest, over his heart.

"I'm not joking, Heather. Think about it. It makes sense for us."

"You think?"

"You and the kids would be able to stay with me, where I could watch over you all. You wouldn't be alone at night or vulnerable to an ex-husband who doesn't know when to quit. You wouldn't have to worry anymore. Not now. Not ever."

She sniffed and shook her head. "I've got to admit you make it sound tempting. But I didn't come here this afternoon expecting a marriage proposal."

Shawn wondered if she could feel his heart slamming in a mad rhythm against her palm. The proposal was more than him protecting her from Adrian. So much more.

"Think about the children."

"I *am* thinking about the children."

He'd made her mad. Why was she mad?

"We can be a family. All six of us, and eventually we can have more of our own, if you'd like, or even keep adopting. The kids love the ranch. They'll be able to grow up here, learn all about raising animals and taking care of the land. It makes sense for us."

She pulled her hand away and dragged it

down her face. He'd never seen her look so bone weary. It pulled at him.

"Can I think about it before giving you my answer?"

"Of course. I'm not trying to pressure you. All I'm asking is for due consideration that you'll take me seriously."

"You've got that. I promise."

"I've got pastor friends in the area. We should have no problem finding someone to hitch us up on short notice."

"Short notice?"

"The sooner the better, don't you think? With Adrian in town, who knows what will happen. We don't want him catching up with you when you're alone."

Way to not pressure her, you jerk.

Shawn wanted to kick himself. If he was trying to scare her off, he was doing a mighty fine job of it. Reminding her that Adrian was a present threat instead of assuring her that he would protect her and the kids.

"Do you have someplace you can stay until we get this sorted out? A friend or neighbor?"

She stood and moved to the coffeepot, pouring herself a fresh cup and then checking out the window on the children before returning to the table. She leaned her hip against the edge of the wood and crossed her free arm over her waist instead of returning to her seat.

"I don't want to impose on anyone like that," she said. "You know how much of a handful the kids can be. Besides, I need to face this." She sounded as if she was trying to convince herself. "I'm not a victim any longer, and it's high time I stopped acting like one."

Was that a *no*?

Shawn's heart twisted as he waited for her to elaborate. Surely she wasn't turning him down, not without taking more time to think about it.

Please. Not a *no*.

"I'm going home."

That was even worse. "Think about what you're saying. It's not safe there. He probably knows where you live." She might not be ready now—or ever—to make a commitment to him, but he wasn't going to step aside and let her walk right into the vortex of danger.

"I'm not an idiot."

"I didn't think you were."

"I'll take every precaution," she assured him. "I'll keep the doors locked and my phone on me. And I'll call the police the moment I see him. Adrian is a mean drunk, but he's only as intimidating as I let him be. He's used to a shell of a woman who won't fight back. I think he's going to be surprised to find that's not who I am anymore."

"He's been in prison. Who knows what kind of man he is now? He could be truly dangerous, Heather. Worse than he was."

"You're right. I don't know what kind of man he is now. But if I run from this, I will be running my whole life. Don't you understand? I can't do this anymore."

"If he shows up at your house?"

"I'll call the police and he'll be arrested. At least then I'll be able to rest easy again—for a while, anyway."

Shawn thought it was a bad plan. The most awful one he'd ever heard, in fact. For starters, he wasn't part of it. And he could count on two hands the number of things that had the potential to go wrong.

And yet—it seemed that Heather had turned a corner. Her weariness and the desperation she'd worn like a cloak for as long as he'd known her had disappeared.

Replaced by determination.

Strength.

Belief in herself.

How could he take that away from her?

She hadn't come here to have him solve all her problems. She'd come to regroup and solve her own. And she had.

He loved her enough to let her see this through, but he couldn't completely let go. He had to do all he could to protect her.

"My number is on speed dial, right?"

She smiled softly. "Number one."

"Good. Don't be afraid to use it. For any reason. Day or night. Whatever you need, I'm your man."

"Thank you for that." She blushed, making her countenance even more lovely.

His pulse heightened, and he wanted to take her in his arms and kiss her senseless, prove he meant every word he said in his proposal. Convince her she really should be with him. It was all he could do to hold himself in check when she brushed the back of her hand against his cheek.

"I'm going to round up the children. It's time for us to go home."

"Heather?" His arm snaked out to capture hers. She turned, an unreadable look on her face.

"Yes?"

"I just wanted you to know…my offer still stands."

Chapter Ten

My offer still stands.

Heather looked in on her sleeping children, tucking their blankets up under their chins and brushing a soft kiss on each of their precious brows. She triple-checked the locks on all the doors and windows and then settled down on the couch with a cup of tea, drawing her legs up beneath her.

Had Shawn really offered to marry her? She couldn't help but feel she'd somehow coerced him into making such a rash proposition. She hesitated even to call it a proposal. Heather scoffed and shook her head.

Adrian hadn't only muddled her life and potentially put her children in danger, but now he was messing with Shawn's head.

Shawn O'Riley didn't deserve to be a part of this drama, and yet in typical Shawn fashion, he'd willingly thrown himself right into the middle of the storm to help her.

He had already changed his whole life around for the sake of little Noelle—and all without a single complaint, which just magnified his goodness and strength.

And now he was ready to embrace her and her children and make them a permanent part of his life for no reason other than to keep them safe. Even though they'd never talked about it, she knew Shawn well enough to know he took marriage seriously. Shawn was a forever kind of guy.

But marriage to her? How could he even imagine it? Of course he wouldn't think of her children as a burden, as she expected most men would. He might worry that he wasn't good enough for them, but he'd never consider them a problem.

But dealing with an abusive and criminal ex-husband and stalker who posed a certain threat to their lives? No one would want to take on that kind of responsibility.

No one but Shawn.

She'd really believed he was joking when he'd first brought up the subject of marriage. A pastor marrying the local divorcée. Yeah—*no*. They would be the talk of the town, and not in a good way. She couldn't imagine how his congregation might respond to him allying himself to her in such a serious and irrevocable way.

Impossible. Outrageous.

But the fact remained that he *had* asked her to marry him—in earnest—and he'd reiterated that offer before she'd left.

He'd even run down a thorough and practical list of reasons why their getting married was a good idea. To protect her from Adrian. To be able to formally adopt all their children. To create a more stable home environment for them.

If she married Shawn and moved to his ranch, the children would all have a mom, the best dad ever, a yard with a fence—split-rail and not white picket, but a fence—*and* a dog. Oh, and however many other animals Shawn happened to be keeping. She'd seen pigs, goats, horses, cats and chickens.

The picture-perfect family.

She choked on her tea.

Marrying Shawn would be anything but picture-perfect. He had enumerated every potential benefit of their possible *collaboration*—except for one, and in Heather's mind it was the most important aspect of all.

Shawn had said nothing about love.

Glaring red flag there. Heather had never imagined she would be in the position of receiving a marriage proposal ever again in her life—nor did she believe she'd ever want one. But a marriage without love?

She'd already been there, and with disastrous results.

Not that there was any comparison. Adrian was all about himself and his own needs and desires. He thrived on hurting people. Shawn never thought twice about willingly sacrificing his own convenience for the good of another person. The proposal itself was just further proof of that.

But marriage?

That was asking too much of him. She couldn't allow him to sacrifice *that* much for her, no matter how tempting it sounded. No matter that his idea—when viewed purely pragmatically—had merit to it.

She couldn't look at marrying Shawn as anything more than a practical consideration even if she wanted to.

The truth dawned on her with such clarity that she couldn't believe she hadn't seen it until now. Her fingers were shaking so fiercely that she was rattling her teacup and had to set it on the table before she spilled the hot liquid on her lap. She placed one palm against her racing heart and the other over her lips.

She couldn't marry Shawn—not because

there was no love between them, but because there *was*.

She was in love with Shawn.

When had it happened? Somewhere along the way Shawn had stealthily tripped the switch that opened her heart to trusting again—feeling again. She didn't just appreciate Shawn for all the things he'd done for her—she had fallen in love with him.

Wow. How had she not seen this one coming?

She'd been preoccupied with Adrian, that was how. She still was—sitting here in her living room, half afraid to sleep for fear Adrian would try to break into the house after dark. Assuming he knew where she lived and that he would slink around in the dark. Adrian's usual MO was to face up to situations right in the light of day and charm his way through them. But prison could have changed him, and she had no way of knowing for sure.

She wouldn't be worried if Shawn were here. His strong arms and warm embrace were her safe spot.

She suddenly wanted to accept his offer of marriage more than anything in the world. Which was, of course, why she couldn't.

A platonic relationship wasn't ideal, and it certainly wasn't anything she'd ever seen in modern America, but it could work. Might work. Maybe—if they were both committed to adopting and raising their children with only feelings of friendship and respect between them.

But living with the man and loving him when he didn't return the sentiment? That was just plain crazy.

Rap. Rap. Rap.

Heather jolted to instant alertness, her heartbeat pummeling her rib cage as adrenaline surged through her.

Was someone at the door?

No, it wasn't the door. At least not the front door.

She must have drifted off daydreaming about Shawn—or rather, mulling over the reasons the two of them could never be together.

What time was it?

She fished the cell phone out of her pocket, but before she could check it, she heard the noise again.

Rap. Rap. Rap.

It definitely wasn't the front door. It sounded like the sliding glass door in the back through the kitchen.

Adrian.

He was here. It was time to end this nightmare.

She dialed the police with shaky hands. As she waited for the emergency operator, she jogged down to the end of the hallway where the kids' rooms were located.

She spoke in quiet tones as she explained the situation to the emergency operator and rattled off her address.

"Please hurry," she ended, hoping she didn't sound as frantic as she felt.

She slipped into Missy's room and scooped the sleeping girl into her arms and then brought her into Jacob and Henry's room and deposited her in bed next to Henry.

"Jacob, honey, wake up." She shook her elder son's shoulder.

"Mama?" he asked sleepily. "What's wrong?"

"That bad man we talked about? He's here. Mama needs to go talk to him. The police are on their way. I want you to watch over your brother and sister. Stay in this room and lock the door when I leave. Don't open it for anyone but me. Do you understand?"

Jacob's eyes went wide but he squared his shoulders and nodded.

"Yes, Mama. I'll take care of them."

"I know you will, my brave boy." She took his face in her hands and kissed his cheek. "It's going to be okay, honey. The police are going to get this guy and put him back in jail so he can't bother us anymore."

She hoped—prayed—that the words were true.

Please, Lord. Watch over the little ones.

She should have listened to Shawn when he'd suggested she not return to her house, or at least she should have found somewhere else for the kids to stay. But she really hadn't believed Adrian would come here. Not in the middle of the night, anyway.

She wouldn't let the regrets take over. The truth was, she was tired of running away. She wanted to confront him and get it over with. If he realized she wasn't afraid of him anymore, he would no longer have any power over her. That moment couldn't come soon enough.

She pressed her cell phone into Jacob's hand. "I've already called the police, but I want you to hang on to this, just in case. Dial 911 for an emergency, all right?"

"Mama?" Jacob's voice was shaky and his lower lip quivered. Heather's heart turned over.

"We're going to be fine, honey." They were. They *were*. She was going to make it happen.

She closed the door and waited until she heard Jacob turn the lock. She wished she believed her own words—that she knew for sure it would be okay. But she didn't know. Only God knew.

She concentrated on evening out her breathing. It wouldn't help for her to hyperventilate and pass out in front of Adrian. He needed to see her at her best so he'd know for certain that she wasn't afraid of him.

She'd come to Serendipity to start a new life, and her nightmare had followed her here.

It was time to put that nightmare to rest once and for all.

She shoved out a breath and turned the corner from the bright living room to the darkened kitchen. She pressed forward, hugging the wall, trying to see outside the glass door without giving her position away. There was no more than a sliver of pale moonlight, just enough to cast ominous shadows across the lawn. She strained her ears to hear anything out of place, but all she could hear was her own breath, which sounded incredibly loud against the silence.

She frantically filtered through her options. Adrian was lurking somewhere around her house. She was fairly certain he'd been trying to open the doors rather than knocking on them, which meant he was attempting to sneak into her house under the cover of darkness rather than announcing himself in the daylight.

But where was he now?

Even if she knew his location, she had no clue what her next move should be.

She wished she'd thought to borrow Queenie from Shawn for a couple days. Having a dog around the house would be a detriment to stalkers.

The police couldn't possibly be far off. She just needed to stay quiet until they arrived and pray that the younger children didn't wake up. They would be so frightened. Poor Jacob had put on such a brave face for the sake of his foster siblings, but she knew he was hunkered down in the bedroom scared half out of his wits.

She despised Adrian for that—for harming her children.

"Heather!"

Adrian's voice sounded as if it was coming from the vicinity of the kitchen window, which she confirmed when he banged his fist against the glass.

"Heather. I know you're in there. I can see you."

Her hair stood on end and alarm skittered like an icy finger down her spine. She struggled to keep hold of her shredding composure.

He yelled and slammed his fist into the glass once again, hard enough to make the pane rattle. That had to hurt his hand, but he didn't flinch. Which meant he'd been drinking. If he kept it up, he'd not only break the window, but he'd wake up the children for sure.

She'd given her cell phone to Jacob, so she couldn't check the time. How long had it been since she'd called the police? Surely they should be here by now. Hadn't they said they were going to keep a cruiser running by her house on a regular basis? Even if they weren't in the neighborhood at the moment, this was a small town. How long could it take?

Where were they?

Adrian had seen her, so there was no sense hiding any longer. She stepped out from behind the wall and looked straight into the window over the sink, glaring at the man who'd single-handedly made her life so miserable.

The face looking back at her through the cloudy, opaque glass reminded her of a dark, fairy-tale version of the evil queen's magic mirror. Adrian's sunken eyes burned into her, his scowl black and menacing. His wild hair and beard combined together to form something truly ghastly.

She should have been terrified. There was a time when she would have been. And though she was not foolish enough to discount the wild-eyed, not-quite-sane reflection in his countenance, she was not afraid.

Not of him. Not anymore.

He reached up to pound his fist into the window again and she didn't even hesitate. He was going to wake up her children, and then she was going to get really angry.

Adrian wasn't here about the children. He wanted her—and he was going to get her. Without considering where her actions would lead, she marched to the sliding door, flipped the lock, flung it wide and stepped through, closing it tightly behind her.

"You want to see me? Well, here I am. What is it you have to say to me?"

She'd heard of people's jaws dropping in surprise, but she'd never literally seen it. Not until now. Adrian was staring at her as if she'd sprouted wings.

"Well?" she challenged, instinctively going on the offensive. "I'm waiting. What are you doing here?"

He stood gaping for another beat before he regained his senses. Then his brows lowered over cold blue eyes.

"No," he countered, his voice low and menacing. He craved fear almost as much as booze, and he was searching for it now. Trying to provoke her. "The real question is what *you* are doing here. Did you really think you could just walk away from me, Heather?"

She had. And she'd been mistaken in that. She couldn't hide from her past. He was staring her right in the face. Icy dread curled around her stomach but she ignored it.

"We're divorced, Adrian. And I have a permanent restraining order against you." She strained her ears for the sound of sirens but heard nothing.

Adrian sneered. "You think a piece of paper is going to stop me, you little piece of trash?"

Heather braced herself. She'd once believed all the names he'd called her. She hadn't seen her true worth until she'd viewed herself through another's eyes. Shawn's eyes. He saw her as God saw her. Her chin rose.

Adrian couldn't take that away from her no matter what he did, but she suspected he was going to try.

He stepped forward, looming over her, using his height to try to intimidate her. She stood tall and maintained eye contact with him. Inside she was quivering, but outside she stood strong.

"You're going to come home with me. Now."

She scoffed. "Not in this lifetime."

Where were the police? What was taking them so long?

The fact that she'd talked back to him appeared to fluster him.

"I'm going to teach you a lesson you are never going to forget," he promised, his voice rising with the excitement of hurting her. He raised his hand to slap her.

"I wouldn't count on that." Shawn stepped out of the shadows, large and aggressive, the brim of his straw cowboy hat pulled low over his eyes. If Adrian was intimidating, Shawn was doubly so.

Adrian took a surprised step backward and pulled his fists up in a defensive stance against Shawn.

Heather had never been so happy to see anyone in her entire life. Not even the police could have topped the relief she felt at the appearance of this cowboy preacher.

"I don't know who you are, mister, but this isn't any of your business."

"I'm making it my business." Heather had never heard Shawn's voice so cold and hard.

"You'd poach on another man's turf?" Adrian asked snidely.

Heather's stomach lurched. That was how Adrian had always seen her. As his property and nothing more.

"I happen to love this woman," Shawn informed Adrian coldly. "I've asked her to be my wife, and will be grateful until the day I die if she accepts me."

"You can't do that," Adrian growled. "I'm her man."

"You're not a man." Heather's throat closed around the words, nearly choking her. "You never have been."

"Shut up," Adrian spat.

"You speak to her like that again and you

won't be standing on your feet," Shawn warned. His voice was low and surprisingly steady, but there was no doubt he meant what he said.

"I can speak to her any way I please. She's my *wife*."

"I'm not your wife," Heather countered, her voice high and strained. "I haven't been for years. You may not want to accept it, but the state does. Get out of my life."

"I told you to shut your trap," Adrian yelled, raising his hand to her once more.

Shawn's fist came out of nowhere, connecting with Adrian's jaw with a satisfying crack. Adrian grunted and went down. Out cold.

Shawn shook his fingers out and shrugged down at the man on the ground. One side of his mouth curled up and he winked at Heather. "I warned him."

"Yes, you did." Heather started giggling and couldn't stop, so great was her relief.

He opened his arms to her and she sagged into him, clutching his shirt, nestling as close to him as she was able. He was so strong. Safe. Steady. She wished she could stay forever in his embrace, listening to the rhythm of his heart, but sirens broke through the silence, and Adrian groaned at their feet.

The police had finally arrived, and Adrian was waking up.

* * *

Heather excused herself to check on the kids while Shawn saw Adrian handcuffed and shoved into the back of Slade McKenna's patrol car.

"Sorry we were late to the party," Slade apologized, crossing his arms over his chest and leaning his hip on the hood of his cruiser. "Serendipity is as quiet as a mouse and just as boring, until it's not."

Shawn grunted. That was for sure. Like when an abandoned baby showed up in a manger at his chapel. Or a hazel-eyed beauty entered his life and turned it upside down and backward.

"We had a bit of an emergency at Jo's house. Her hip gave out again. You'd think after all the surgeries she's had that the doctors could keep her on her feet."

"Is she okay?"

"Sure. You know Jo. She wouldn't let anyone fuss over her, and taking her to the hospital was completely out of the question. But she does like drama. She had everyone on duty at the fire department, all the paramedics, the cops and Dr. Delia swarming around her house like bees."

"With Jo as the Queen Bee," Shawn guessed.

"Exactly. So it took me and Brody a minute to unravel ourselves from her when the call came in. Of course, once she understood the situation,

Jo was the first one pushing us out the door. We came as fast as we could."

"It's all good. I was here before Adrian got too far out of hand."

Slade laughed. "Yeah. It looks like you saved the day. Nice work, you decking him, Pastor. I would've done the same."

"I'm not a fan of physical fighting," Shawn admitted. "But I'm not ashamed of what I did tonight. The jerk was about to slap Heather. That's not going to happen while I live and breathe. Not ever."

"He won't be here to bother her again anytime soon. He violated his parole by coming here, so he's going straight back into the can."

"I'm glad to hear it. Heather has enough on her plate taking care of her kids without having to worry about Adrian lurking about."

"Hopefully he'll learn his lesson this time."

"I'm not holding my breath. He's not beyond the Lord's help, but that's what it's going to take to get through to him."

"How did you know to be here, anyway?" Slade asked, his lips quirking into a lazy smile and his eyes gleaming with amusement. Shawn could see he already had his own theories as to the reasons Shawn might be near Heather's house so late at night.

Shawn still held out hope that Heather would

accept his marriage proposal, but whether she did or not, he didn't want anyone spreading gossip about her reputation.

"Nothing shady, I promise you," he said, shoving Slade lightly.

Slade laughed.

"No, really. Jacob called me. Heather had told him to watch over the younger kids and keep the bedroom door locked. Apparently she gave him her cell phone. He got kind of freaked out and called me. I came running."

"Yeah. I'll bet you did."

"Yes," Shawn agreed, narrowing his eyes on Slade. "I did."

"Just teasin' you, buddy. It's all good. I'm glad you were here."

"Shawn?" Heather called, returning to the sliding glass door. "Did you want to come in for a bit? I've got Missy back in her own bed and Jacob all tucked in. And I just made a fresh pot of coffee."

"Pour me a cup, will you? I'll be right in," Shawn replied, before turning to shake hands with Slade. "Thanks for your help."

"You've got it. Tell Heather I'm sorry we didn't get here sooner."

"Will do."

Shawn dragged his fingers through his hair as he stepped through the door and slid it closed behind him. He was still experiencing a mild sense of unease and he wasn't sure why. Adrian was going to jail. Heather and the kids were safe.

All's well that ends well, right?

And then, there it was—the lingering problem. All *wasn't* well for him. Not until Heather answered his question. Would she agree to be his wife?

The present threat was over and Adrian was on his way back to prison, but that didn't change a thing as far as Shawn was concerned. He would marry Heather yesterday, if he could. Or tomorrow. Or next month, or next year, as long as she said *yes*.

He found Heather on the sofa in the living room, her legs pulled up beneath her and a mug of coffee in her hand. She'd set another mug on the opposite side of the table next to the armchair, but Shawn slid it toward Heather and sat down right next to her with his arm across the back of the couch.

She wouldn't even look at him. She sipped her coffee in total silence, her gaze fastened on the black liquid in her mug. The easy camaraderie they'd shared just minutes earlier had vanished, replaced by an uneasy tension.

What was she thinking? He waited for the

silence to prod it out of her, but she was stubbornly quiet.

"Heather, honey, talk to me," he said at last.

"I guess I should thank you for rescuing me." She laughed, but she'd never sounded so apprehensive before.

How could she think he was waiting for an expression of gratitude? Didn't she know him at all?

"There's no need for that, you know. Of course I came when I was called. I would have been there earlier if I had known. I'll always be there for you."

"Wait—what? I didn't call you."

He chuckled and brushed her hair back behind her ear with the pad of his thumb. "Not directly. Jacob did."

"Jacob? I gave him my phone, but I didn't expect him to use it."

"Mmm. I'm glad he did. Poor kid was frightened half out of his mind."

"I didn't know whether I should wake him up or not when Adrian arrived. I should have thought it through better and left him sleeping. I've probably scarred him for life."

"Naw. Don't beat yourself up about it. I made sure he knew he was a hero for protecting his brother and sister—and protecting you by calling me."

"But I want him to be able to be a child as long as possible. I feel like I've ruined it for him, forcing him to man-up before his time."

"Boys appreciate a little responsibility. He got the chance to show you that you can depend on him. That's a good thing."

"I'm still taking him out for ice cream tomorrow."

Shawn chuckled. "Sounds good. I'll buy."

She made a tortured sound from the back of her throat. "Shawn."

Concerned, he narrowed his gaze on her. "What is it, honey? Talk to me. Please."

She smiled at him, but there was so much agony in her eyes that it went straight to his gut, knife-sharp and stinging. She brushed the back of her fingers down his jaw as if it were the last time she was going to touch him.

Tension rippled through him as he waited for her to speak.

"Adrian is on his way back to prison."

Right. Nice to know, but not exactly news. "Yes. And?"

She still refused to look at him, her gaze going no higher than his mouth.

"And you don't have to pretend anymore." The words came out in a rush, stumbling over each other.

"I'm sorry?" What was the woman talking about? How was he pretending?

"It was so sweet of you. You'll never know how much I appreciate your help. Really. And I understand why you said what you said to Adrian. But now it's just you and me, and I'm letting you off the hook, so you can relax."

She was *letting him off the hook*? What did that even mean?

He filtered through recent events, trying to figure out what he'd said to Adrian that Heather believed hadn't been entirely truthful. From what he could remember, there hadn't been many words in their altercation. Mostly it had been his fist on Adrian's face. Nothing dishonest about that, as far as he was concerned.

"You want to tell me what you're talking about?" Maybe if he had a hint.

She seemed to shrink into herself. "You said you loved me."

Why did she make it sound as if he'd said that he thought she smelled like apple cider vinegar?

"Yes," he agreed. Not like this was some great revelation, either. "I did. And?"

"I understand why you said it. But now that it's over—well, I just don't want you to feel obligated to continue the charade."

What *charade*?

"I feel like I've missed something," he admitted, running a hand across his jaw.

Something major, apparently.

"I know why you asked me to marry you, Shawn. And that makes you the best kind of man there is. I'll never be able to find words to tell you what that means to me. You were ready to sacrifice everything for me and the kids."

"Well, of course I was. Am," he corrected himself, frowning.

The woman wasn't making sense. What good was a husband if he wasn't willing to sacrifice everything, even his own life, for his wife and children?

"I want to thank you, and tell you I appreciate it."

"You already said that."

"But it's over."

Over? After everything that had happened, she could just walk away from what they had together? Or had he been so wrapped up in his own emotions that he hadn't realized she didn't return the sentiment?

He reached for her chin, gently tipping it his direction so she had no choice but to look at him.

"Are you trying to tell me you don't love me—that there's no chance you ever will?"

Her eyes widened to epic proportions. Her mouth moved, but no words came out.

"I—I—" she stammered, trying to turn her head away, but he wouldn't let her, not holding her with his hand, but with his gaze.

"You…what?"

"I love you."

He nearly sagged with relief, but his love for Heather flooded through him, bringing every nerve ending to life.

"That's good to know."

"But I don't see how that changes things."

Shawn shook his head. "Woman, if you don't stop talking in riddles, you're going to send me right off the deep end of crazy."

"I love you," she reiterated. "I can't deny it. But you don't love me, and I can't live like that. I thought about it—a lot. But I can't. I just can't."

"But I said—"

"That you loved me. Under duress, to protect me from Adrian. I get it. But I'm not holding you to it."

"I did not say I love you under duress."

"What do you call it, then?" She didn't allow him to answer, but answered for him. "I call it self-sacrifice. Thinking of other people before yourself. And I applaud you for it."

"Okay, I'm obviously slow, so you're going to have to lead me to water by the nose. I asked you to marry me. So how is it that you don't think I'm in love with you, exactly?"

She laughed through her teeth, a dry hiss. "You didn't say so when you proposed, for starters."

"What do you mean I didn't—" He stopped dead in the middle of the sentence as the realization hit him like a bullet in the chest. "I didn't." He rubbed his hands down his face and groaned. "I didn't, did I?"

Heather drew back.

He slid off the sofa and crouched in front of her, framing her face in his hands. "Honey, I'm an idiot. Forgive me."

Her hazel eyes clouded with tears and Shawn felt like the biggest dolt in the world. He'd clumsily trampled over her feelings and now was at a loss as to how to undo his mistakes. He'd already caused her enough pain as it was.

"I'm so, so sorry. I was busy trying to prove to you that I could keep you guys safe, and then I go and neglect to mention the most important thing of all—that I love you."

Hope flared in her irises, burnt orange turning gold, the color of sunrise.

"In my defense, it wasn't that I forgot to mention it, exactly. I am so crazy in love with you that it was a given in my mind and I thought it was written all over my face. For some reason I believed it was coming out of my mouth, when clearly it wasn't. My heart was doing backflips when I asked you to be my wife."

She rubbed her lips together as if they'd suddenly become dry. She ran her hand over his eyes, down his nose, over his jaw, as if she were trying to memorize his face.

"I blew it before, but hear me now. There is nothing in this world I want more than to put a ring on your finger. Not because I have to, but because I want to. I offer my protection, yes, and my provision. But most of all I offer you my heart. You and the children. You're already my life. I hope I can be yours."

She stared at him but didn't speak.

He couldn't swallow around his emotions. Love. Hope. Fear of rejection.

"You don't have to answer if you're not ready. And I know I pushed you too hard earlier today about setting a date. I was thinking about Adrian's threat to you, but he won't be bothering you any longer. We can take our time. Just—just please don't say no without thinking about it."

She smiled then, and to Shawn it felt like the swelling of a symphony. "You silly man. You think I'm going to turn you down?"

"Well, you did say—"

"That was only because I thought you were

asking out of a cockeyed sense of obligation to me."

"Oh, I'm obligated, honey. Obligated to kiss your pretty lips. Often and thoroughly. I'm obligated to say 'I love you' instead of rattling off my to-do lists. Obligated to give you my heart and my life." He lowered his head to hers, hovering just above her lips. "But there is one thing I need from you in return."

She wrapped her arms around his neck. He'd never felt anything quite as perfect.

"Name it," she whispered. "It's yours. *I'm* yours."

"Yeah, that's the thing," he said back, kissing her, and then kissing her again. "You never really answered me."

Their foreheads met and she smiled into his lips.

"Then I'm answering now. *Yes.*"

Epilogue

Rap. Rap. Rap.

Heather's pulse jumped, but it wasn't because someone was knocking on the door, or even because of who was on the other side.

Today was the day.

"Heather? You about ready?"

When Heather turned in her bustle to move to the door, Alexis gave a little squeal of distress and launched herself for the train of the white gown. Heather had thought a different color might be more appropriate, but Shawn had talked her into white. She had asked her new friends from church—Samantha Davenport, Mary Bishop and Alexis Haddon to stand up with her today.

"Sorry," Heather said as she giggled, swinging the door open. They were tucked into one of the Sunday school rooms for final preparations.

Shawn's father beamed back at her. Six months sober and counting. He was still in rehab but had come out for the wedding today. To their delight, Kenneth had come clean after Shawn had called to tell him of the engagement. He'd said he wanted to be there for all of his grandkids, and so far, it appeared he was serious about the endeavor.

"Shawn sent me to tell you that curtain call's in fifteen minutes." He wagged his eyebrows. "You're certain you're ready to get hitched to my son?"

"More than you could ever imagine," she assured her soon-to-be father-in-law. "Is everything good to go on the other end?"

"I don't know about that," Kenneth said with a laugh. "Shawn's practically jumping out of his skin, he's so anxious to tie the knot with you. I'm afraid he's going to pass out from too much adrenaline. You don't happen to have a paper bag on you, do you?"

"Sorry, no."

"Just teasing, love. I'll get him to the altar, don't you worry none about that."

"I appreciate it." She smiled. She hadn't really been worried. "Tell Shawn I'll see him soon."

Meeting Shawn at the altar couldn't come soon enough for her. She'd been dreaming about this day for months now. Shawn had insisted she plan every little thing. She would have been happy with just the two of them standing up in front of one of his pastor friends, but he'd insisted she have a "real" wedding, whatever that was. He wanted everything to be perfect for her on her special day. Before she knew it she was caught up in colors and caterers and floral bouquets.

All she cared about was having a real *marriage*, and she knew she was going to get that with Shawn. She was glad, though, that they'd waited, if only because the extra time meant she'd had the opportunity to start attending church, reacquainting herself with old friends and neighbors and meeting new ones.

They were all out there now, waiting to see their beloved pastor marry the love of his life. She supposed it was about time she made that happen.

It was only when she stood in the vestibule just outside the sanctuary that her nerves kicked in. She was more than a little anxious about stepping on her dress and falling on her face in front of everyone, but not a bit worried about joining her life to Shawn's.

There was no fear in love.

Samantha and Mary helped Henry, in a little white tux with his blond hair carefully slicked back, start up the aisle bearing the pillow on which their rings were bound. Next went Missy in her precious red flower-girl dress and carrying a basket of rose petals. Shawn had insisted on roses—it was the only real opinion he had on the wedding details other than the color of her dress.

With final giggles and well wishes, Samantha, Mary and Alexis drag-stepped down the aisle. Heather strained to see if she could catch a glimpse of Shawn, but he was standing off center and she couldn't see him. She knew once she looked into his eyes all would be well in her world.

She carefully released a breath and smiled at Jacob, who was pacing the vestibule and looking uncomfortable in his classic black tuxedo. Like Henry, he'd slicked his dark hair back, but a stubborn lock fell over his forehead. Jacob, like his future father, preferred life in jeans and boots to dressing up, but he was trying to be a good sport about it. Just for today.

"Ready to do this?" she asked him.

The boy's eyes gleamed. He stood tall and offered his arm to Heather.

"You look beautiful," he murmured with an awkward grin.

"And you, sir, are unbelievably handsome. I'm so proud to have my son walking me down the aisle today." The three children's adoptions were set to be finalized just after the first of the year, but in Heather's heart it was already a done deal.

The bridal march started and the congregation rose. Heather scanned the room, seeing a tidal wave of the joy-filled faces of her friends packing the entire sanctuary. The place was full to overflowing. Standing-room only.

Nerve-racking.

Thank You, Lord, for seeing me to this day, but please don't let me trip over my dress. Or my feet. Or my tongue.

She stepped into the aisle, straining to see Shawn. Where was he?

Fresh Christmas trees with twinkling lights from Emerson's Hardware lined the outside walls and poinsettias graced the altar, creating an intoxicating mixture of scents. The Christmas season would always carry a special place in their hearts, even without their anniversary falling deep in December.

Shawn stepped forward, into the middle of the aisle, and reached out his free hand to her. In the other he held Noelle, who'd grown considerably over the past few months. She was saying simple words and was near to taking her first step. Her little red dress matched Missy's, and she had roses threaded through her black curls.

Shawn's gaze met hers and she forgot to

breathe. He was handsome in his work clothes—khakis and dress shirts—and even more so in jeans and boots and sporting that straw cowboy hat of his. But today, in a classic black tux and bolo tie, his black boots polished and shining, he was magnificent.

She reached his side and he wrapped his large, warm hand over hers. Kenneth took Noelle and deposited her into her birth mother's arms. Kristen had made a full and complete recovery, a blessing the doctors could not explain. She was now enrolled at a community college and had a job and an apartment, all of which Shawn and Heather had helped her acquire. It was wonderful and satisfying to see the teenager get on her feet. She'd asked—begged—for them to adopt Noelle, and so they'd met with a lawyer to see about an open adoption. Kristen visited them on weekends to get to know her daughter, and they were happy to have her.

After all the years of not wanting to wake up in the morning, Heather now couldn't wait for each day to begin. Holding the hand of the man she loved, surrounded by her family and friends, every day was an adventure, every second filled with love and joy.

The ceremony was kind of a blur to her. She couldn't think. She could only feel—overpowering love and emotion for the man standing at her side. She didn't hear a word anyone said until it was time for her to turn to Shawn so they could speak their vows to each other. He recited his vows to love and cherish her in the stout, persuasive voice of a natural-born orator, but she didn't need his words to be convinced.

He proclaimed his love for her with every smile, every gesture, every expression. And when she looked into his eyes, she could see forever.

* * * * *

Dear Reader,

What do you get when you combine rugged cowboys with adorable babies? Why, my new series, of course! I'm so excited to present Cowboy Country, where we'll adventure together back to Serendipity, Texas. If you've read any of my previous Serendipity novels, you may catch a glimpse of some familiar characters.

In *Yuletide Baby*, Heather and Shawn were both survivors of wretched pasts and victims of others' bad choices. When their pasts come back to disrupt their lives, they are only able to overcome and triumph with God's help and by turning to each other.

Most of us battle some memories we'd rather forget. If you're struggling to reconcile your past with your present circumstances, I hope you'll be encouraged by Shawn and Heather's story and, with God's help, look to your future with renewed hope. God's mercy is new every morning.

I hope you enjoyed *Yuletide Baby*. I love to connect with you, my readers, in a personal way. You can look me up at www.debkastnerbooks. com. Come join me on Facebook at www.facebook.com/debkastnerbooks, or you can catch me on Twitter, @debkastner.

Please know that you are daily in my prayers.

Love courageously,

Deb Kastner

Questions for Discussion

1. Why do you think Shawn believed he was unqualified to care for Noelle? What changed his mind?

2. Why do you think Noelle's mother left her at the church? Was it an act of love or selfishness?

3. In what ways, practical and spiritual, did the community step up to support Shawn, Heather and the foster children? What are some ways you can offer your support to someone in need?

4. How did Heather's abusive past affect her self-image? Has your self-image been impacted by any event or person? Was it positive or negative?

5. Why do you think Shawn continued to own his ranch even after he became the pastor of a church?

6. Why do you think Heather felt guilty about Adrian's driving accident?

7. Did you relate more to Shawn or Heather? Why?

8. How did David's accident affect Shawn as an adult?

9. Do you think Heather will ever be completely free of the trauma Adrian caused her?

10. In what ways was Noelle a blessing to Shawn?

11. Why do you think Missy's accident shook Shawn's faith in himself as a foster parent?

12. Why do you think Heather hesitated when Shawn proposed to her?

13. What are some of the challenges Shawn and Heather had as single parents? How will this change when they become a blended family?

14. What made you pick up this book? Title? Author? Cover?

15. Does this novel have a takeaway value? Can you define it? Does it apply to your life?

LARGER-PRINT BOOKS!

GET 2 FREE
LARGER-PRINT NOVELS
PLUS 2 FREE
MYSTERY GIFTS

Love Inspired ® SUSPENSE

RIVETING INSPIRATIONAL ROMANCE

Larger-print novels are now available...

YES! Please send me 2 FREE LARGER-PRINT Love Inspired® Suspense novels and my 2 FREE mystery gifts (gifts are worth about $10). After receiving them, if I don't wish to receive any more books, I can return the shipping statement marked "cancel." If I don't cancel, I will receive 4 brand-new novels every month and be billed just $5.24 per book in the U.S. or $5.74 per book in Canada. That's a savings of at least 23% off the cover price. It's quite a bargain! Shipping and handling is just 50¢ per book in the U.S. and 75¢ per book in Canada.* I understand that accepting the 2 free books and gifts places me under no obligation to buy anything. I can always return a shipment and cancel at any time. Even if I never buy another book, the two free books and gifts are mine to keep forever.

110/310 IDN F5CC

Name	(PLEASE PRINT)

Address		Apt. #

City	State/Prov.	Zip/Postal Code

Signature (if under 18, a parent or guardian must sign)

Mail to the **Harlequin® Reader Service:**
IN U.S.A.: P.O. Box 1867, Buffalo, NY 14240-1867
IN CANADA: P.O. Box 609, Fort Erie, Ontario L2A 5X3

**Are you a current subscriber to Love Inspired Suspense books
and want to receive the larger-print edition?
Call 1-800-873-8635 or visit www.ReaderService.com.**

* Terms and prices subject to change without notice. Prices do not include applicable taxes. Sales tax applicable in N.Y. Canadian residents will be charged applicable taxes. Offer not valid in Quebec. This offer is limited to one order per household. Not valid for current subscribers to Love Inspired Suspense larger-print books. All orders subject to credit approval. Credit or debit balances in a customer's account(s) may be offset by any other outstanding balance owed by or to the customer. Please allow 4 to 6 weeks for delivery. Offer available while quantities last.

Your Privacy—The Harlequin® Reader Service is committed to protecting your privacy. Our Privacy Policy is available online at www.ReaderService.com or upon request from the Harlequin Reader Service.

We make a portion of our mailing list available to reputable third parties that offer products we believe may interest you. If you prefer that we not exchange your name with third parties, or if you wish to clarify or modify your communication preferences, please visit us at www.ReaderService.com/consumerchoice or write to us at Harlequin Reader Service Preference Service, P.O. Box 9062, Buffalo, NY 14269. Include your complete name and address.

LISLPDIR13R

ReaderService.com

Manage your account online!
- Review your order history
- Manage your payments
- Update your address

*We've designed
the Harlequin® Reader Service
website just for you.*

Enjoy all the features!
- Reader excerpts from any series
- Respond to mailings and
  special monthly offers
- Discover new series available to you
- Browse the Bonus Bucks catalog
- Share your feedback

Visit us at:
ReaderService.com